Underneath the Moon

6

DAN HOLT
and
MAX HOLT

Published by:

MaxHoltMedia

DAN HOLT & MAX HOLT

OTHER SCI-FI BOOKS BY DAN HOLT
Underneath the Moon
Underneath the Moon 2
Underneath the Moon 3
Underneath the Moon 4, with Max Holt
Underneath the Moon 5, with Max Holt
Keepsake
Sleep Mode
(The above releases are also on Kindle and Audio, via Audible.com)

OTHER SCI-FI BOOKS BY MAX HOLT
Alien Planet
Series - AI Rising (Book One) THE DOME, with Dan Holt
Intended future releases –
   AI Rising (Book Two) ANDROID REBELLION

DAN HOLT & MAX HOLT

Cover design by Max Holt Media, with Eddie Holt
Proofread assistance by Carla Bower

ISBN: 13: 978-1-944537-37-1

Published by: Max Holt Media
303 Cascabel Place,
Mount Juliet, TN 37122
www.maxholtmedia.com
On facebook at www.facebook.com/maxholtmedia
        Email – max@maxholtmedia.com
        Twitter - @maxholtmedia

DAN HOLT & MAX HOLT

CONTENTS

Prologue		9
1...Spaceport Zeta		13
2...Incoming		31
3...Cosmos		53
4...R & R		59
5...Found		63
6...The Concavian		71
7...Arrival		85
8...The World Tour		95
9...The Calling Card		107
10..Launch		115
11..The Vortex		121
12..Spaceport Arrival		133
13..Procylon 2		141
14..Friends In Need		147
15..Birthplace		153
16..Sailing On		155
17..Parking		175
18..The Way Station		181
19..Trappist 1		199
20..The Star System		205
21..Concavia		209
22..Contact		221
23..The Hollow World		225
24..Home		239
About the Authors		247

DAN HOLT & MAX HOLT

PROLOGUE

300,000 Years B.C.

The rogue ship exited the wormhole vortex, 44.5 lightyears from where it had originated. As they entered the yellow star's solar system, a scan of its planets confirmed no presence of intelligent beings.

"**Commander Gahntor...destination, sir?**"

"**Third planet from the star!**" the stoic starship commander instructed his pilot. "**A perfect star system for our plan.**"

"**Yes, Commander.**"

Two starships had launched from their home planet following a meeting with the planet's scientific hierarchy. The majority of scientists had voted to seed the planet Zannia with a specific DNA, designed just for that experiment, which was intended to produce intelligent beings of an unusual size. Gahntor and a colleague had disagreed. They saw an opportunity with this research project to create a 'servant force' with warrior capabilities, enabling their planet's influence to spread and permeate the galaxy. However, the scientific community had always resisted anything militant in their seeding of planets. Unable to get approval to create a servant planet, Gahntor and his colleagues spirited away the pattern statue, carved to illustrate the intended outcome of the experiment. Along with it they stole sever containers of the amber life-giving fluid necessary for the DNA experiment to evolve into sentience. Gahntor's sister ship, transporting the amber fluid, had taken a secondary route to avoid suspicion. Unknown to Gahntor, fate had destroyed the secondary ship when its shield failed, allowing a projectile, a few centimeters across, traveling at light speed, to pass through the ship, destroying the life support system, and killing the crew. The dead ship, with its cargo of amber fluid, would drift aimlessly throughout the galaxy.

As Gahntor's ship approached the dark side of that distant world, atmospheric penetration brightened the night sky over the mountainous landscape. Several small invertebrate creatures retreated into their burrows.

The commander selected the best location, ordered the landing, and established a temporary base camp made of stones from the surrounding landscape. Then, he waited for the second ship's cargo of amber fluid. After some time, Gahntor realized that the essential fluid would not be arriving. Leaving the pattern statue behind as a marker, he secured the base camp and launched to search for the missing ship.

"Approaching the vortex, sir."

"Bypass it. Steer direct through Quadrant Four. Proceed at Power Level Six. We must locate the missing ship and return with the catalyst."

The Navigator beseeched the commander. **"But, sir, Quadrant Four is still 60 percent concentrated with debris from the Orion supernova. At Level Six, the chances are great that..."**

"Then do your job...NAVIGATOR! Navigate around the debris. If we are to be successful, we must have that fluid!"

The renegade commander then pushed the pilot from his seat and took the controls. He dialed in **POWER LEVEL 6** on the Engine Power Panel, placed his hand over the large button and pressed, **ACTIVATE**.

A glowing mist enveloped the ship and it instantly disappeared into Quadrant Four of the Milky Way Galaxy.

DAN HOLT & MAX HOLT

Chapter 1

SPACEPORT ZETA

Present Day

Spaceport Zeta, hanging alone in space, has a secret. The combined crew of giants and humans, manning Starship Omni-Star has been looking for that secret...a destination that could finally reveal the truth about where they came from and who they really are.

In their past space explorations, they had made many amazing discoveries. But what they were about to find would push them to the edge of understanding. Some will be enlightened. Some will disbelieve. But all will be astounded.

Once they find their destination, the space-hardened crews will use their skills and determination to succeed in this, their most important journey. They all sense that the **something** they are looking for in Spaceport Zeta's massive library has been beckoning them inward, deeper into the Milky Way Galaxy.

The ship that would ferry the anxious crew toward the unknown, sat in its mooring, loaded and ready. While the crew searched for answers, there was another set of eyes, watching their every move and searching for an opportunity.

The Citizen

The alien's smooth grey skin and his small size aided his attempt at stealth. Inside Zeta's massive hangar bay there were many dimly lit recesses in which to remain hidden. His familiarity with the spaceport enabled him to locate what he was looking for in only two hours. Now, he had found it. He glanced at his digital arm-panel to confirm the name:

USS OMNI-STAR

He then peered from his hiding place...YES, the glistening starship was indeed the one.

His initial plan, to become a stowaway, was thwarted by the spaceport's security system, with its surveillance cameras and the perpetual guard detail.

"It's been long enough," he thought, *"all these years here, waiting; that's punishment enough!"*

He looked back at the small device, swiped his bony finger across the starship's name and saw the next piece of the puzzle in his plan; the Starship Captain...**Colonel James Austin.** The alien smiled. If the rumors were true, he knew this commander would not give up in his search. It was a unique characteristic of the Earthlings.

The grey-skinned hand closed the lid, deactivating the device. *"I must quickly find a way to approach this commander, for I know they will soon find what they are looking for. Those humans and their giant comrades seem dedicated enough to trek 44.5 lightyears deeper into the galaxy. But, if the questions they are asking about their origin are to be answered, there is the only place they will find them...my home. Whatever it takes, I must be on that ship."*

The Omni-Star was continuing crew rotations as per the clock and ship's regulations. Many, having done their duty, were anxious to get back to touring the marvelous creation floating in space, the spaceport, the awesome accomplishment of the Zylons many centuries ago.

Some wondered if there was ever a time when the Zylons, like the human *little ones* of Earth, had a small tinker-toy-looking configuration of latticework construction circling their planet every 90 minutes, forever weightless, forever floating, and totally dependent on frequent visits from the planet below. Earth's first space station would hold only a few souls that bravely volunteered to sacrifice their health to learn the limits of human tolerance. They, as all do, soon learned that the humanoid must have gravity to maintain wellbeing, health, and functionality. To remain long in space, they had learned that one must bring their own oxygen, gravity, and atmospheric pressure.

No sun ever rose or set on Spaceport Zeta. It was continuously bathed in starlight from all directions. Each of the volunteer staff, all the visitors, and traders in passing, brought their own sunrises and sunsets with them, in the form of their own timekeeping. Every timepiece in the spaceport was set according to the cycle of its owner's home planet. Planets are jealous of their own. Each starship is an extension of its home world.

Once again, the now 'off duty' crew of the Omni-Star filed off the ship for a new adventure. However, a contingent of researchers was on duty in the library, focused on their mission. They could not allow anything to delay its accomplishment.

The Library

Colonel Austin was touring with the Omni-Star's Bridge Crew; first officer-Bruce Wilson, Sheldon Darcy-pilot, Timothy Dalton-copilot, Katherine (Katy) Baylor-computer control, Sharon Milla-flight safety, and Melvin Faulkner-telemetry and navigation. After a few minutes, the transport stopped, and they exited at the entrance to the library. They stood, looking across the sea of information, with the scientists from Earth in many of the cubicles, busily studying the available information on the neighboring star systems and their planets. They were so involved sifting through the documents, visuals, and recorded information that they weren't aware of others around them.

They were beginning their third week in the library, totally dedicating themselves to locating a destination that had promise of being the Moai's home base. If they found anything resembling the Moai, the stone giants of Easter Island, it would be an indication that living giants were there…or had been there. They felt sure they would find what they were looking for. It was just a matter of time.

Colonel Austin also noted that the 50 astronomy graduates that had accompanied the mission scientists, were scattered throughout the library, still searching for a common foundation to enable one engaged in astronomy to view a star-system and make an educated guess of its probability of harboring life. Astronomers had been *guessing* about life on other planets for centuries. Here, at Zeta, the answer was obvious. However, a new way to search from a distance for the elements of life would be invaluable. He admired their persistence; they indeed had the stuff of astronomy.

Jimmy and his crew walked back to the transport where Seven, their android driver and guide, sat completely still, like a statue. Their movement activated the android's system, and he was instantly responsive. The machine was so sophisticated and well programmed that it was difficult to distinguish it from human, or humanoid. What an accomplishment, a level of sophistication that must have been a thousand years in development.

"Seven," Colonel Austin said, "do you know everything that's recorded in that library?"

"No, Colonel. My system has a need-to-know filter to keep from overloading my internal memory. There's a lot of information in the galaxy. A brain the size of this space station would not hold it all. But I can easily research anything with just a title or key word only."

"That makes sense."

The crew boarded the transport. "Seven," Jimmy said, glancing at his communicator to check the time, "take us to the dock. I'm supposed to meet the giants' commander, Mentar, and his crew. He's going to transfer his personal shuttle to the Omni-Star. They will be joining us on our quest."

"Mentar is going with us instead of Kronos?!" Bruce exclaimed.

"Yes," Jimmy said. "Mentar just made the final decision and the change this morning. As the days have passed since he made the decision to send Kronos and a team, he and Kronos decided it would be only fitting that Mentar go with us. Since Mentar has spent a lifetime getting his people back to an orderly civilization with a home planet of their own; he should have the honor of joining us to find our common origin. Mentar admits he had been haunted to know the answer."

"I'm glad," Bruce said. "The adventure and the answer are his."

"It's also ours as sentient brothers," Jimmy added with feeling.

Jimmy nodded to Seven. Seven activated the transport and began a journey to the lower parts of the spaceport, then to the hangar bay where the starships were moored. When Jimmy and crew arrived, Mentar's pilot was just hovering Mentar's personal shuttle from Little One, the giants' Starship, over to the Omni Star. Mentar greeted Colonel Austin, then the two of them and their combined crews watched the 160-foot shuttle move slowly into the hangar bay. The doors closed majestically as if capturing something special. Jimmy wondered, *"The next time those doors open and the shuttle powers up and exits, what kind of world will be below and what kind of mystery will be waiting?"*

Minutes later, Mentar's pilot came down the ramp of the Omni-Star and joined the group. Kronos had picked a team of four for the voyage aboard the Omni-Star. Mentar had given them the nod. He introduced them to Jimmy and his crew. Mentar's pilot would be Bayan. Jimmy recognized him from the many shuttle trips on Zannia, the giants' home planet. The copilot was Vennvar, a seasoned pilot from Zannia's spaceport, ferrying crews to and from the planet's radio telescopes and the space elevator. Navigator, Yaanmar, was the third backup crewmember from Starship Little One. And Safety Officer, Winnievaar, was a female instructor on Starship Dynamics at Zannia's university. She had taken a leave of absence for a tour on Little One to this Spaceport. It was a unique opportunity to accompany Mentar on this voyage, a chance of a lifetime. She notified the university that upon her return she would be lecturing on the results of this venture for the benefit of all Zannians.

Mentar's team and Earth's human *little ones*, awkwardly, shook hands all around. There was something special about the camaraderie. Winnievaar extended just her index finger to Colonel Austin. He had long since gotten over the anomaly of forty-foot-tall giants living and working with humans, the *little ones*, as the giants had named the Earthlings. He smiled as he attempted to close his hand around the end of her finger and *shake her hand*. Holding the end of her finger momentarily, he searched her face for frivolity. There was none. She was all business and radiating excitement.

Lilah Owenby, the teacher bound for the human colony on Zannia, garnered the crew's assistance to move her belongings and equipment to Starship Little One. Back on Earth, she had been selected by educators to be the first official headmaster of the Earth Colony School on the giants' planet. Her grandparents, Jack & Brenda Owenby, founders of the colony, anxiously awaited her arrival. She had accompanied the Omni Star crew from Earth and was changing ships to finish her journey to Zannia, where she would begin her new job.

Brad Givens, the two-centuries-old cowboy, was also changing ships to complete his journey on the same ship to Zannia. He had been rescued from a dead Altiarian ship, found drifting in space near the Omni Star's path through the Kuiper Belt. Its crew had been killed when an undetected space object had penetrated their shields and destroyed their life-support system. The cowboy was the only survivor, because he had been placed in suspended animation by the crew.

Contact with Altiarian officials determined that the ship had been missing for 230 Earth years. Its mission had been to abduct living creatures on other planets and study their anatomy for research purposes. Brad Givens had been abducted from the saddle on his horse, riding along the Red River in Texas in the late 1800s. A search of his downline family tree determined that his only living relatives were a great-great granddaughter and her son who had volunteered to be Zannian colonists. The cowboy was given the choice of returning to Earth or continuing to Zannia to be with his only known family. His choice would soon reunite him with his family on Zannia.

Brad thanked Colonel Austin for the rescue, the orientation, and finally, the special effort to locate his family. He had talked to his great-great-great grandson, living on Zannia, via the Quantum Communications system. However, it had turned out to be a short conversation. The awkwardness of the situation gave them both a loss for words. Understandably so. What they needed was time to adjust and get to know each other. It would come. After all, they were family.

Kronos, at the helm of Little One and fully boarded for the journey home, said his goodbyes to Mentar's team and the *little ones*, and then gave the order. A cargo ship from the Spaceport Zeta fleet was waiting outside to accompany Little One to Zannia and pick up a load of Zolaadine ore and return it to the spaceport, to be added to their *Ship's Store*. The spaceport's Logistics Office felt it would sell well to other planets, since the added strength of the new metal would enable them to build their own orbiting space stations. It was Zannia's first outer-planet trade deal, one that

Mentar had previously arranged. Little One, slowly and majestically, left its mooring and made its way to the spaceport exit to begin its three-lightyears trek to Zannia. Aboard, the young scientists from Zannia were all mentally richer for having had the experience of Spaceport Zeta.

There were moments of silence as Mentar watched the last of the bulk of the starship clear the exit through the magical curtain of inert gasses, separating Zeta's habitable atmosphere from the harshness of open space. It was almost like he thought he would never see that ship or its crew again.

Jimmy broke the silence. "Mentar, as you can see, this is one of their modified shuttles, with accommodations for those of us of different sizes."

Mentar smiled and nodded.

Jimmy continued, "I would like for you and your team to join us on our tour. Is there any particular place on the spaceport you'd like to see?"

As Mentar and his team joined them on the transport, he looked down at Jimmy. "Yes, let's go down to Research and Development and see how they are doing on our robot, Zolaadine Man. Ever since we discovered him after the forest fire on Zannia, I've been curious about how he was made and *when* he was active on Zannia. I checked with them a couple of days ago and they had his power circuits repaired but they've seen no response yet. They said there were hundreds of tiny circuits that were fried when the machine experienced a powerful energy surge. It was most likely hit by something like a laser blast."

When they arrived at the transport, Seven, was standing near the wall, conversing with another android that had just wheeled a large container into the area. Seven was signing for the contents. He turned when he saw the group approach the transport.

"Ah, Colonel, the new translators have arrived."

The devices looked like clip-on identification badges, except they were one-inch thick and covered in small holes, much like audio speakers. They were in two different sizes; one was two inches square and the other about 8-inches-square. These would accommodate the smallest and the largest of Zeta's visitors.

Jimmy and the others peered into the large crate. "Translators?"

"Yes, sir. Our Technology Division has been working on their development for some time. Zeta is the chosen destination of more and more species of space farers. We no longer have sufficient androids to handle the translation needs and the digital translation tablets have proven to be too slow for most conversations. These clip-on devices are programmed to automatically translate any known language into your chosen language. Colonel, use the digital readout on the back to select English. Mentar, select your Zannian language."

Jimmy and Mentar each picked up one that was their size. They both selected their language. When they clipped them on, the devices sensed the application and automatically turned on. Then he looked at Mentar, *"Say something in your language."*

Mentar looked somewhat puzzled. He took a breath and said a phrase in his Moon Language, the language of Zannia, first heard by Earthlings on the Moon decades earlier.

Jimmy heard, coming through the clip-on device, an android-sounding translation from Mentar, in perfect English. Mentar had said in his native language: *"If these devices work, it will save us a lot of time."*

Jimmy, having heard his friend's voice in perfect English, smiled and replied, "Well, my large friend… looks like we are going to be saving a lot of time."

Mentar smiled when he heard the perfect Moon language translation coming from his larger device. All the others quickly lined up to receive their translators. Jimmy called the bridge crew and informed them to alert all crewmembers to report as soon as possible to the hangar area to pick up their translators.

Finally, Seven called for the team to board the transport and then began the miles trek to Research and Development in the lower parts of Spaceport Zeta.

Riding along on the transport, Mentar turned to Jimmy. "Colonel, how are your scientists doing in the library; anything promising yet?"

"Not yet. They are combing through records systematically and have been for about two weeks now. This library contains records of every star-system in this spiral arm of the galaxy, plus those up to a hundred light-years deeper inside. That's a LOT of records."

Mentar nodded. "It's a difficult task to find something without a name; going by shape only."

"Yes, it is," Jimmy agreed. "Hats off to those guys for taking on the task."

"Perhaps you should suggest they take a break for a couple of days and give it a rest. There are two theaters in the spaceport. I went to one while we were waiting for you to arrive. They are excellent. Their internal food replicators have even produced an Earth snack in honor of your crew's return. I believe it is called popcorn. I tried some but those puffy little nodules kept getting lost between my teeth."

Jimmy laughed. "Not a bad idea, Mentar, I'm sure just the smell of the popcorn will draw us *little ones* to visit when our mission allows. I'll suggest that when we check on them later. With the new translators, I guess movie subtitles will be a thing of the past."

Seven drove the transport into the doorway of the Research and Development section. He stopped the machine and communicated with an android sitting at a desk near the entrance, then turned. *"The robot is down one floor and to the right in the electronics lab. Follow me."*

The group disembarked the transport and followed Seven to an escalator which took them down a floor. They then took a right and proceeded through an arched doorway. Zolaadine Man was sitting on a table, looking straight ahead. Made from the Zolaadine ore, his twenty-foot-tall medal body glistened. His leg, originally hit by a laser, had been repaired. When the group entered, he turned and looked at them momentarily, then his gaze went up to Mentar's face, then back to looking straight ahead.

"He is active!" Mentar said.

A tech stepped away from his computer terminal, approached the group, and spoke: "We're getting there. He had dozens of damaged circuits that had to be traced and restored. His memory is basically intact which is amazing, considering the surge that went through him when the laser hit occurred. By the way, the team that repaired his leg said the laser that took it off was an industrial model, not a weapons grade laser. It was designed for cutting, probably to work whatever they made from Zolaadine. He had a buffer, a protection circuit, on his main core. That helped a lot. He should be fully functional in a couple of days. When all his circuits are complete, we'll update his programming."

"Excellent work!" Mentar said. "Please notify me when you've finished."

The tech nodded then returned to his computer analysis.

"Those guys are good!" Sheldon said as the group exited the lab.

"I think you have to be to get here," Jimmy said.

"No doubt," Mentar agreed.

"Mentar," Jimmy said, "he was damaged by an industrial laser. That changes the picture. He may have been around during the building of Zannia 2, the escape-ship your ancestors built when the planet was dying."

"We can find that out when he's ready to be examined."

Midway back to the library, four of the transports, with the 50 astronomy graduates on board, passed by, heading for the Aisle Side Restaurant. They were taking their lunch break an hour earlier than the scientists that were searching for the Moai's origin. It was simple logistics, not to overwhelm the eating establishments. They waved as usual.

Upon arriving at Aisle Side, Amil Lajahda and Connie Singleton, exited the transport and looked for a table. They usually had lunch together as they had become partners in their information research. Amil saw Meta, the Lindian girl they had met earlier, sitting at a table alone. He pointed her out to Connie. "Let's see if we can join her. I would like to talk to her."

Amil approached her table. She looked up, recognized him, and smiled. Amil gestured toward the other chairs at her table. The Lindian smiled and nodded. Amil signaled their transport driver. He came to the table. "Could you translate for us?"

The android held up a hand. He stepped to the transport and came back with three of the new clip-on translators. He handed one to each of them and showed them how to select their language. Meta smiled when she found hers on the list. They all clipped them to their collars, and they turned on.

"*These will translate for you,*" the android said. It then sought out the other astronomers and issued their translators.

Amil looked up at Meta's large crystal-clear blue eyes. "I'm glad to meet you again. I'm Amil Lajahda; this is my colleague, Connie Singleton."

Meta, surprised at the efficiency of the translation, spoke up. "I'm Meta Levaine. These new translators are amazing. Thanks for stopping to have lunch with me. Let's order and then we can talk."

After they finished their electronic order, Meta asked, "Did you find what you were looking for at the information station?"

"Yes," Amil said, "we did get some important stats that, when compared to the rest of our research, could yield some very important guidelines on studying the heavens."

The dinner entrées arrived promptly. As they enjoyed the food, idle conversation began and Amil outlined his vigil to get through school and get aboard the starship for this opportunity. He told of his childhood dream of being an astronomer and his family's sacrifice to help him. Then he mentioned his promise to his mother. He looked Meta in the eye: "I want to find something that would have come from the stars, something special for her."

Meta smiled and nodded. "The best place to search for something like that is the barren moons of planets. When a supernova happens, the stars' gravity attracts the debris. The moons get in the way and act as catchers of the debris."

"Our solar system has 173 known moons!" Connie interjected. "I never thought about searching there for parts of the cores of the stars."

Meta opened her waist pouch, a purse of sorts, and extracted a sphere the size of a golf ball. It was crystal clear, slightly oval in shape, with a blueish vein running through it. It was nearly weightless. She handed it to Amil. "My father found several of these on the smallest of Lindia's three moons. He was there prospecting for Neodymium."

"It's beautiful," Amil said. "Is it a diamond?"

"No. We were unable to match it to any known element. We call it Starlite. My dad gave them to me."

Amil handed it to Connie. She examined it, then handed it back to Meta. She handed it again to Amil. "Give this to your mother."

Amil slowly extended his hand and accepted the prize, then looked up at Meta. "Thank you. I will give it to her. She will treasure it. I'm going to tell her about you, the girl I met among the stars. May I take your picture?"

Meta nodded. Amil handed his communicator to Connie and positioned himself beside the Lindian, held up the starlite crystalline sphere, and smiled. She looked over at him, turned toward Connie, and smiled as well.

DAN HOLT & MAX HOLT

Chapter 2

INCOMING

The transport slowed and stopped at the entrance to the library, delivering Colonel Austin, Mentar and their teams to check on the progress of the researchers, looking for the needle...or planet...in the haystack.

Jimmy placed one foot out of the vehicle and looked at Seven. "Thanks for the ride. We will be here for a while. I'll let you know when we need to return to the Omni-Star."

"Yes, Colonel, just call me."

As Jimmy got out of his seat, a deafening alarm blasted throughout the corridor, accompanied by bright flashing red lights mounted overhead, spaced 50 yards apart in both directions. Jimmy was so startled that he almost fell onto the floor. Mentar had already dismounted and momentarily placed his giant hands over his ears. Some on their teams had looks of instant panic. After ten seconds, the piercing alarm reduced to half-volume and was accompanied by a calm but loud android voice. With the new translators, everyone heard in their own language.

RED ALERT, RED ALERT…INCOMING OBJECT. LEVEL ONE DANGER. ALL ZETA PERSONNEL REPORT TO YOUR EMERGENCY STATIONS. ALL VISITING PERSONNEL REPORT TO YOUR SHIPS. DO NOT ACTIVATE YOUR PROPULSION SYSTEMS UNTIL INSTRUCTED TO DO SO. ALL PILOTS AND STARSHIP COMMANDERS, REPORT TO THE COMMAND CENTER FOR INSTRUCTIONS. THIS IS NOT A DRILL.

The audible alarm silenced but the red lights continued to flash. The doors to the library burst open as those inside began to hurriedly exit. The corridor quickly filled with loaded transports and hundreds of others walking. The Earth researchers gathered around Jimmy, expecting some answers.

Jimmy looked at Seven. "Can you find out what this is all about?"

"Just a moment, sir." Seven calmly stepped to a computer access point, about six feet square, mounted on the wall. He folded down a flat glass panel, void of any controls. He placed the palm of his right hand on the glass and the screen brightened with a message that no one understood. Seven touched an icon and selected ENGLISH from the list. He then looked at Mentar. The giant glanced at his team and then nodded. Over the years, the giants had learned both the spoken and written English language. The message then read: ACCESS GRANTED. After he touched several more points on the screen, a graphic display appeared. He placed his hand at the edge of

the screen and began to swipe to the left, repeatedly. He stopped at an image and then placed both hands on the screen and spread them apart. The image enlarged until it filled the screen.

Jimmy and Mentar moved closer, staring at a schematic of Zeta, hanging in space. Lines from each side of the space station curved out to an object on the opposite end of the screen. Jimmy squinted. "What is it?!"

Seven drew a circle around the object with his finger and enlarged it. They were looking at a large comet...and it was headed straight for Zeta. A dotted line curved from the center of the comet to the center of Zeta. Beside the line were the words: PROBABILITY OF IMPACT...100%.

Jimmy turned and looked at the faces of those gathered. They weren't looking at the comet; they were looking at him. His mind went briefly back to a NASA classroom, ten years earlier, when he was in EMERGENCY ACTIONS class at the Starship Commanders' School. He remembered one statement by the instructor:

*"Knowing what to do in an emergency is critical. Equally important is bestowing on your crew the confidence that you **know** what to do."*

Jimmy looked back at the approaching comet, then addressed Seven loudly, "How long before impact?"

Seven touched another ICON. A digital read-out appeared...displaying a four-digit number. Seven stared for a moment. *"The comet will impact Zeta in three days, eleven hours, and twenty-seven minutes."*

The colonel looked at the researchers and his crew. "Okay, Mentar and I will be accompanied to the meeting by the ship's navigator and all shuttle pilots. The rest of you, return to the ship and make initial preparations for departure.

"Katy, contact our DOE shuttle pilots and make sure they heard the alert and know to meet us at the Zeta Command Center."

"Yes, sir."

Seven arranged for transports to return the crew and researchers to the Omni-Star. He then transported Jimmy, Melvin Faulkner and Mentar, along with his shuttle pilot to the meeting. As they entered the Command Center, Jimmy noticed that most of the crews and commanders of the 18 visiting starships were already assembled around a large oval table, which was raised 15 feet above the floor, to accommodate those of different sizes. Jimmy and crew climbed the stairs to take human-sized seats. Mentar's crew took giant seats on the floor nearby.

There were several digital countdown clocks on the table, displaying several different renditions of timekeeping. Jimmy's seat was near the one displaying Earth-time.

As he looked around the room, he saw that all attendees were wearing the new translators. In a few minutes, the Zeta staff entered and took seats near a raised podium. The Spaceport Commander went straight to the stage.

"Thank you all for your prompt response to the alert. The projected impact time of the comet is displayed on various time-keeping systems throughout the room. The newest members of Zeta are our friends from Earth and Zannia. They both use Earth-time and measurements. So, I will be using these numbering systems during this briefing. Your translators will automatically convert the numbers for you.

"Now, let me give the details we have before you ask questions. Over the years, our Automated Tracking System has catalogued over 100,000 of the objects that wander around the galaxy and pass in the proximity of Zeta. Our last close call of an impact was over a hundred Earth-years ago. However, fifteen minutes ago, our ATS alerted us that a comet, designation…Q2317-Alpha, passing through the edge of our star system, abruptly changed course, increased velocity and is headed straight for us. It is estimated to be a two-billion-ton ball of ice. On its current trajectory, we only have…uh," he studied a view-panel in front of him, "…looks like three days, eleven hours, and three minutes."

A starship commander across the table interjected, "Commander, if you have been tracking this object all these years, how did it catch you off-guard? Comets don't just change trajectories on their own."

"This one did. Our security analysis teams are investigating. Since comets don't do that on their own, there's obviously a cause."

A commander near the end of the table abruptly stood, interrupting the Zeta commander. He cleared his throat, still staring at a portable computer system. All eyes were on him as he slowly looked up at the Commander.

"Uh, sir, I am Daka Palaton from the Gladdon System. I think I can explain the unusual behavior of this comet." He glanced back at his computer and then at the others in the room. "Ah...I think we caused the comet's course change."

The room was silent for a moment. The Zeta Commander spoke, "Ok, Commander Palaton, explain what you mean."

"Sir, as you are aware, we are from Gladdon Four. For the past ten years we have been suffering from a severe drought. For years we have been harvesting ice from passing comets to irrigate our fields. With the drought worsening, we decided we would capture Q2317-Alpha, since it is so huge, and divert it to an orbit around our planet, so we could harvest all of it." He glanced at the screen again. "I've just been informed that the propulsion system our crew buried inside the comet has malfunctioned and is now out of control."

Another commander stood. "But Daka, many of us in this room are from planets that harvest comet ice. It's a routine procedure. What went wrong?"

The Gladdon commander shifted nervously on his feet. His grey skin turned a lighter shade. "Well, our crew attached an S-27 Fission Rocket as the propulsion system. After ignition, it malfunctioned and went to its full-throttle setting. It is not responding to control commands. We can't shut it off and we can't change its trajectory."

There were gasps around the room.

Zeta's Commander stared for a moment. "Commander, you know well that the S-27s were outlawed five years ago as unstable and unreliable. Can you explain why your planet would violate Federation law?"

"Sir, I can't speak for our governing body, but I was told they wanted to use up the S-27s we had in stock. I'm guessing it was a financial decision."

"Well, unless we come up with a quick solution to this rogue comet, your fleet may be harvesting space debris from what WAS Zeta." He turned back to the room. "What we need now is a plan." He turned to the android assistant behind him. "How many individuals are here at the spaceport?"

The android reported, *"17,216."*

"How many are visitors?"

"11,739."

"Okay, they can evacuate in their own ships. If all pods are serviceable, how many staff will the escape pods hold?"

"4,000."

"My Command Ship will hold 500, so that leaves… uh…"

"977, sir, including androids."

"So, how many of your ships can give a ride off this metal ball?"

Every commander raised his hand.

Mentar spoke, "Commander, since my planet, Zannia, is the closest to Zeta, I will offer haven to any in need, for as long as it takes."

"Thank you, my giant friend. I understand Zannia is a pleasant place to be. But before we pack our bags, let's see if Zeta can be saved."

There were some low rumblings as starship commanders conferred with their pilots.

Snyder and Abbott, the DOE shuttle pilots from the Omni-Star, were seated behind Jimmy. Snyder leaned forward. "Colonel, Abbott and I did it before. Maybe we can do it again."

Jimmy nodded and then stood to address the leader. The room quietened as the others listened for his suggestion. "Commander, the two pilots behind me have changed the direction of a large comet before. They are Omni-Star's DOE shuttle pilots."

"DOE pilots? What's a DOE?"

Jimmy glanced around at the mutual confusion on the group's faces. Faces that were in the crosshairs of an oncoming monster. Omni-Star's commander realized that this was a time for some diplomacy. "D.O.E. stands for Defenders of Earth. Our engineers designed two special dual engine shuttles, doubling the power, armed them with twin laser cannons and low-yield neutron torpedoes for just such a contingency as this."

Jimmy motioned Abbott and Snyder to stand beside him. "'This is Captain Benjamin Snyder and Captain Gregg Abbott. Years ago, when one of our ships was in route to Zannia, these two pilots were able to use the DOEs and their lasers to prevent the collision of our ship with a large comet. I think they may be our best shot at saving Zeta, although this comet is overwhelming in size. They would like to try. The DOE shuttles are kept stocked and loaded and could be underway in…say…30 minutes. With your permission, Captain Snyder here will describe the best approach to diverting the comet."

The Commander nodded.

Captain Snyder stepped closer. "Well, sir, two billion tons is a big one. We would need for the Gladdons to transmit their data base to us, with details of both the comet and the S-27. Abbott and I will set our shuttles on course for the comet and proceed at maximum speed. Based on your schematic, we can be there in less than a day. We will then use our lasers to disable the S-27. That will stop the acceleration, which will give us a little more time. Next, we will attempt to laser-cut the comet into manageable chunks; pieces that we can nudge off course with Zeta. We should be able to get all that done in a day. That leaves another day for you to determine if the remaining debris can be weathered or if Zeta will have to be abandoned."

There was silence in the room. After a few awkward moments, Jimmy spoke: "Uh…sir, unless someone has a better idea, I suggest we get started."

The Commander nodded. "Yes, Colonel. I see no other solution being offered." He turned back to the group of starship commanders. "Okay, the Omni-Star's powerful shuttles will launch as soon as possible. The Gladdon Commander will data-transfer the information they need. All starships will house their crews on board and be in a state of readiness to depart with just an hour's notice. The Zeta crew will maintain their emergency alert status and begin to shut down non-essential equipment. All Escape Pods will be inspected and serviced as required." The Commander stared straight ahead, as his brain ran through the checklist. He looked up. "Gentlemen, you know what to do...you are dismissed."

Comet Q2317-Alpha

Snyder watched the two-billion-ton ball of ice grow larger and fill his view out the windshield. He keyed his radio, "Man! That is one big icicle!"

Snyder agreed, "Yep...looks like maybe ten times the size of our first one. I'll take the right side; you take the left. Let's fly the whole length, looking for natural flaws we might use to break this thing apart."

Abbott agreed. "OK, sounds good. The schematic they data-fed us shows the S-27 to be dead center in the back, buried 500 feet deep in a hollowed-out tunnel. Let's be sure to stay out of the engine's fission ion trail...that would fry our ships."

"Roger."

Both DOEs traversed the huge hunk of ice until the ion trail became visible. They saw several large cracks in the comet that were potential laser targets to dissect it after disabling the engine in the S-27. They couldn't use the torpedoes because the explosions would just create a massive debris field of lethal ice chunks.

At the back end, they hovered and analyzed the wayward engine spewing a mile-long trail of 3,000-degree ions. Snyder keyed in. "This is going to be a problem. The tunnel is not wide enough to get a ship inside and still avoid the ion trail. I don't see how we can get close enough to get a shot at the S-27."

Abbott moved a few feet closer. "Yeah, I see what you mean; better tell the Colonel this will take longer than expected."

Zeta Spaceport
Communications and Control Center

The Zeta Commander, Colonel Jimmy Austin and Mentar were staring at the large view-screen depiction of the comet and the two DOEs. Computer updates of the radar images every second created a moving real-time image of the approaching disaster. Jimmy glanced at the Distance-to-Object readout. It was still over 21 million miles away.

All starships, with their crews and passengers aboard, were nervously awaiting word from the Command Center. Those who could sleep were getting some rest; most could not. All escape pods were serviced, powered up and ready for launch.

The radio activated, breaking the silence. "Zeta Spaceport, this is Captain Snyder, calling for Colonel Austin."

Jimmy keyed the mic. "I'm here Captain, go ahead."

"Colonel, this is one big chunk of ice. The Gladdons buried the S-27 deep in a tunnel too small for us to get in. We can't get a shot at it. We'll have to cut the back part off, then nudge it off course and let the S-27 take it out into deep space. Then we can cut the rest into manageable chunks and take them off course too."

The Zeta Commander looked at Jimmy. "How long with all of that take?"

Jimmy keyed in. "What's the expected timeframe?"

"Just a minute, sir." After conferring with Abbott, he came back on. "Sir, we think we can get all that done in another day or so."

Mentar looked at the Time-to-Impact readout. "That will only give us an 18-hour cushion."

Jimmy nodded and keyed back in. "Roger, Captain. You two do the best you can and keep us informed."

The pilots maneuvered the two DOEs to opposite sides of the comet, about a thousand yards from the back end, and began making a laser cut around the circumference of the comet. They updated Zeta at the four-hour mark and made another call at the eighth hour.

"Zeta Command Center, this is Captain Snyder in DOE Number One. We are at the eight-hour mark and we've almost cut through to remove the rear chunk of ice with the S-27. When it breaks loose, we will...uh...wait, uh...something is wrong with the S-27...it's glowing white-hot! I think it's gonna ...oh, my Go...."

The radio signal went dead...followed by nothing but static. The Command Center crew stared at each other. Jimmy keyed the mic. "Uh, Captain Snyder, this is Colonel Austin...are you there?"

There was just the static.

"Captain Snyder...come in please."

Nothing.

"DOE Number Two, Captain Abbott, do you read me?"

"Look", said Mentar.

Jimmy joined the others staring at the radar screen. There were thousands of huge ice chunks...all headed for Zeta. The two DOEs were not distinguishable among them.

15 Million Miles from Zeta

DOE Two was tumbling end-over-end with ice chunks bouncing off its surface. Both rotor pods were off-line, and Abbott and crew were struggling to regain control. When the unstable S-27 exploded, most of the force went their way and sent them hurtling through space. In those moments, there was just static coming from the radio.

Snyder's DOE was pushed ten miles out from the comet, with no obvious damage. His power and systems remained intact; except he had no radio contact. He quickly regained control and made a call. "Gregg…are you okay?"

He heard nothing. He stopped the outward drift and engaged the forward thrust of both rotor pods. The ice-debris field was widening, so he pulled the nose up and navigated around the growing cloud of ice. When he rounded the cloud, his radar picked up Abbott's DOE, fifty miles away, tumbling at 500 miles an hour. "Hang on!" he shouted to the crew and engaged full Power. In a few minutes he had a visual on DOE Two. "Gregg, Gregg….can you hear me?!"

Finally, after another burst of static. Abbott answered. "Yeah, Ben, we're Okay. I got one pod back and they're working on the other one. I almost got the tumble stopped. I need you to rendezvous with me and check my ship for damage."

"Roger, almost there."

After Abbott stopped DOE Two's tumble and drift from the comet, Snyder flew circles around the ship to assess the damage.

"Okay, Gregg, you're banged up a little with some big dents, but I don't see any hull penetrations. Check your laser."

Abbott fired two laser bursts. "It's okay, Ben…still works."

"Alright, let's head back to the comet…what's left of it, and see what we need to do."

After surveying the aftermath of the explosion, Snyder called Zeta with the bad news.

"Colonel Austin, this is DOE One calling…over."

"SNYDER! Thank God you're alive. What about Abbott and his crew?"

"Gregg Abbott here, sir…we're banged up a little but we're back online and ready to work."

"Great…glad to hear it. Captain Snyder, what's the situation?"

"Well, sir, the bad news is…the explosion shattered the comet into thousands of pieces…most of which look like small rocks…nothing Zeta can't handle. But we can see at least a hundred pieces about the size of a battleship. No way you guys can withstand those."

"Is there any good news?"

"No, sir. The *really* bad news is that the debris headed your way was accelerated by the explosion. We are near full power just to keep up with them. They're headed toward Zeta at a million miles an hour."

There was a deafening silence in the Command Center. The leaders were just staring at each other. Mentar turned and read the countdown clock. The computer had automatically adjusted for the increased speed of the debris. "Fourteen hours and seven minutes," he read.

Zeta's aging Commander turned and slowly surveyed the Command Center, and then looked at Colonel Austin. "It will take a hundred years to rebuild

Zeta. This part of the galaxy will suffer from the loss of this way-station."

The others didn't respond…there was nothing they could say.

The Commander sat at his position, flipped the intercom switch, linking all spaces inside Zeta and to all starships.

"ATTENTION ALL PERSONNEL. THIS IS THE ZETA COMMANDER. THE DOEs WERE UNABLE TO DIVERT THE INBOUND COMET. IN FOURTEEN HOURS, ZETA WILL NO LONGER EXIST. I HEREBY COMMAND ALL STARSHIPS, SHUTTLES AND ESCAPE PODS TO ABANDON SHIP…I SAY AGAIN…ABANDON SHIP. THIS IS NOT A DRILL."

He released the switch and sat back, just staring ahead. Mentar headed for the door with Jimmy following. Just before exiting, the giant stopped and stared back at the countdown clock. "Wait a minute," he said. Jimmy watched as the giant walked back to the Command Console and keyed the mic. "Captain Snyder, this is Mentar. Can you use the DOEs' lasers to reduce the size of those large chunks?"

"Uh…yes, sir, but all that will do is create over ten thousand small pieces, still on course for Zeta at a million miles an hour. No way the spaceport can handle them all."

Mentar keyed, "Standby."

Jimmy had moved closer. "What are you thinking?"

Mentar turned. "The Waddle Cone on the Omni Star. It generates a shield that defends the Omni-Star from space debris when we traverse space at high speeds. Why can't we take the Omni-Star, engage the Waddle Cone, and plow a trail through the ice debris?"

Jimmy paused only seconds, "Yes, that will work!"

The Zeta Commander interrupted. "What do you mean. Is there a way to save Zeta?"

Jimmy explained. "The Waddle Cone was invented by the Zannian engineers. It transmits an envelope of energy around the ship to prevent small space debris from penetrating the hull at high speeds."

"You mean, like a shield?"

"Exactly. However, we've never tried it on debris this large. Those chunks of ice may be right on the edge of the Cone's capability. But I feel it is worth a shot."

The spaceport commander stared for a moment. "For a chance to save Zeta, I'll take that chance."

Mentar looked back at the Time-to-Impact. "But, if it's going to work, we need to launch, like, right now."

Jimmy keyed the mic. "Snyder?"

"Go ahead, Colonel."

"We think we can save Zeta with the Omni-Star's Waddle Cone. Can you get those pieces down to refrigerator-size or smaller?"

"Consider it done, sir."

Jimmy keyed the Zeta Intercom link directly to the Omni-Star. "Attention crew; all personnel disembark now. Zeta will arrange for your escape on other ships. Mentar and I will fly the Omni-Star into the comet's debris field and use the Waddle Cone as a wedge to deflect the ice away from Zeta. It will be a rough ride and I don't want to risk my crew. We will launch in 30 minutes. Is that understood?"

After a moment, Bruce's hesitant voice responded. "Roger, Colonel...understood."

There was an awkward moment of silence. The Commander stuck out his hand to each of them. "Thank you. I will wish...or as you Earthlings say...pray, for your safety."

Mentar smiled. "I think you better pray for the Waddle Cone. We have never had it under such stress before. This will be a chance to test it."

Seven took them to the hangar bay and stopped the transport at the ramp of the Omni-Star. *"Best of luck gentlemen."*

Jimmy shook the android's hand. "What about you, Seven, how are you getting off this ball."

Seven practiced an Earth smile. *"I'm not."*

Mentar looked at him. "But you must!"

Seven continued. *"The Commander has decided to stay behind and wait for you to save the station. He said that if you can brave the danger, so can he. I am his assistant...where he goes...I go."*

Jimmy nodded. "I understand loyalty...it's what every commander desires from his crew." He shook his hand again.

Seven gripped it firmly. *"Good luck."* Then, he drove away.

Jimmy and Mentar walked up the ramp and onto the Bridge. They were startled by the entire crew, still there, standing at attention. Before Jimmy could say anything, Bruce Wilson stepped forward and saluted. "Colonel, you are the commander, and we are your crew. If you succeed, we succeed. If you are in danger...so are we. Where you go, we go...uh, sir."

Jimmy looked at Mentar; he displayed a giant smile, and a nod. He looked back at his crew. "Okay," he said, "let's get this baby on the way."

Upon Zeta's instructions, all starships in line to exit, moved out of the way for the Omni-Star to depart. The Zeta Commander announced. "ATTENTION ALL EXITING SHIPS AND PODS. THE OMNI-STAR WILL ATTEMPT TO DIVERT THE COMING ICE DEBRIS AWAY FROM THE SPACEPORT. ALL PILOTS... PROCEED TO A POINT A THOUSAND MILES FROM ZETA AND HOLD FOR FURTHER INSTRUCTIONS.

Time to Impact:
Six hours, seventeen minutes, eleven seconds....

The Omni-Star moved to a position between Spaceport Zeta and the oncoming shattered comet. With the Waddle Cone fully engaged, she began accelerating toward the cluster of ice projectiles. There seemed to be a strange *glow,* they had never seen before, emanating from the hull of their ship when the safety officer turned the Waddle Cone generators to maximum. The leading edge of the debris began to bounce off the Cone's forward projection.

Jimmy looked around at the crew. "Tighten your belts, folks. This is going to get rough." He keyed the radio. "DOEs One and Two...thanks...you've done your job. Now, proceed at least a thousand miles out of the way."

Snyder keyed, "Uh...roger, sir...good luck."

"Abbott here, sir...looks like your closing speed with the major debris-field is two million miles an hour...God speed."

Mentar and Jimmy glanced at each other as the radar showed they were about to hit the gigantic center mass of the ice debris. Jimmy hoped the crew couldn't see him gripping his arm rest. Slowly, the ship began to vibrate, as the Cone's bow wave was compressed by refrigerator-sized chunks. Soon, there was a solid wall of tumbling ice-chunks bouncing off the energy field and wedged out into space. Mentar pointed at the Hull Vibration Readout...it was at 91 percent. Neither leader mentioned it out loud. At one point the vibrations were so severe that Bruce couldn't read the instruments. The whole crew was silently sweating.

After an hour of a white-knuckle ride, the vibrations began to subside. Finally, the Omni-Star broke out of the debris into clear space. There were cheers and high-fives on the bridge.

Jimmy keyed the radio. "Zeta Command...the Omni-Star is still in one piece! We made it through!"

The Commander answered. "Roger, Colonel, we can see a 500-mile-wide tunnel in that ice cloud. You did it, we are all breathing again! Zeta owes you a debt of gratitude."

Jimmy smiled at Katy Baylor and keyed the mic. "How about some free drinks at the Spirits and Song Pub?"

"That, sir, will be yours! Today the party is on the house."

"Roger, Commander, we appreciate that. We are now reversing course and returning...for the party."

DOE's One and Two merged with the Omni-Star's flight path and flew escort on the way back. The Commander radioed all ships and Pods to radar-track the debris and return to mooring after all was clear.

That night, there was a celebration like none before. The swirling smoke from the free drinks created a blue cloud on the ceiling of the Spirits and Song. The respect shown to Jimmy, Mentar and their crew by all other starship crews put them firmly in the family of *hardened space travelers.* Their reputation would last for generations.

DAN HOLT & MAX HOLT

Chapter 3

COSMOS

Planet Earth
NASA headquarters – Frank Gordon Spaceport

NASA headquarters, now located at the Spaceport in Wichita, Kansas, was in constant contact with all ships on mission status. Clifford Russell, NASA administrator, reviewed his daily log of the Quantum Communications terminal. The Omni-Star was still at Spaceport Zeta searching the archives for some necessary information to further pursue the quest of finding the origin of humanity. As time passed, planet Earth settled down, realizing that it could be a long quest that could take years to conclude.

The Omni-Star, while originally on her way to Spaceport Zeta from Earth, had radioed back the information on another chunk of space debris that had threatened the solar system. Starship Cosmos had promptly taken care of it. Since then, all had been quiet. Impressed with Cosmos' capabilities, thousands had applied for space duty, all vying for a position on the starship. Many landed positions on the smaller interplanetary ships: Discovery, The Maxie Gene, and The Mary Lou. These ships were proactive in the development of Mars, the ongoing project that would span several lifetimes as they brought the red planet back to a shirt-sleeve dwelling place with very forgiving gravity. Eons ago, the giants were brilliant in constructing a retirement destination on this smaller planet, with its lower gravity-well. Because of that, much of the infrastructure was already there and could be restored.

Further, the three smaller 600-foot diameter interplanetary ships alternated on training missions out to Saturn space, to the abandoned ship, Zannia 2, now known as a moon of Saturn and given the name Lapetus. That now-empty 900-mile-diameter sphere, the Zannians ancient escape ship, had become a training tool. The new space cadets would suit up, enter, and explore the craft. It was valuable training to ready them for starship duty, should the opportunity come their way. That mission alone, training in Saturn space, was a reward that would last a lifetime.

The dome over Cydonia on Mars was nearing completion. Initially, it would house those that were working on terraforming the red planet. Some of the giants were already talking about retiring there someday.

Cosmos was outfitted with a complete crew and was ready to sail the seas of space. Ongoing training, since the Omni-Star had launched, had readied Cosmos' crew for the challenge.

The next step for the crew of the starship was wormhole qualification. Colonel Austin had communicated with Earth daily concerning the quest in

Zeta's library and any progress that had been made. All knew that one day there would be a breakthrough and the quest would be on.

Clifford, the Frank Gordon Spaceport Administrator, entered the Comm Room and had the tech enter the appropriate code for Jimmy's communicator. Jimmy, being at Spaceport Zeta where the wormhole training was available, could make the arrangements. Despite the staggering distance, the colonel answered in less than a minute. The tech energized the system and nodded to the administrator.

"Colonel," Clifford said, "we have Cosmos staffed with fresh voyagers and prepped for flight. What we need to happen next is to get these people trained for wormhole travel. Since it's likely that you and the Omni-Star, on your mission, will be away from Earth for some time, I think the thing to do is to have the team that trained your crew handle Cosmos' wormhole training as soon as they are available."

"Earth is now a member of the Alliance; they will provide the training," Jimmy said. "We could have the android team meet you at the vortex there in the solar system and then provide the classroom training onboard ship. At the same time, the crew of Cosmos will be able to use the wormhole to travel to Zeta for their in-tunnel training. That way, they will get to experience the Spaceport here. While in the tunnel, the training crew of androids will do an additional 7-day seminar, which, in this case, will be from the vortex there to here and back to the solar system. You could simply add a couple of days here for their introduction to Spaceport Zeta."

"My thoughts exactly," the administrator agreed. "The vortex is three months travel time from Earth for us since we are inside the solar system. Let's see if the trainers will be able to schedule a rendezvous at the vortex for the training exercise."

"I'll check and let you know when that training exercise can be arranged here," Jimmy said, and then disconnected.

He immediately approached Seven and explained the circumstances for Cosmos and petitioned for the training seminar. Seven communicated with Command Central for a few moments, then responded to Jimmy. *"Tell Cosmos' commander to go ahead and fly the mission when ready and notify us one month before arriving at the vortex, then again one week out. We will be able to work with that."*

The administrator notified the new commander of Cosmos, Colonel Leslie James Stahls, the grandson of the silver haired, 109-year-old, Senator Roger Stahls. The doctors said, regarding the Senator, that the 26-year sleep in suspended animation on the Moon, the miraculous time out of aging, gave the centenarian the extra years. He had married early in his career, was still healthy, and still serving in congress. As a matter of fact, he was the longest serving senator on record.

The young Colonel Stahls immediately ordered the ship to make final preparation for launch in one week. He inherited a seasoned bridge crew who had been serving as backup on Cosmos' previous mission to Zannia and back, by way of Spaceport Zeta. Since spacefaring was an around-the-clock business, they had logged many space-hours at the helm of the starship. They had seen several emergencies and knew how to handle them. Leslie himself had studied the logs on those emergencies at length. His bridge crew knew their business; he had total confidence in their collective ability. His pilot, David Walters, copilot, Angie Baker, computer control, Walter Feldman, flight safety, Henry Alderman, and telemetry and navigation, Berniece Whitley, all knew the godsend of the wormhole system, having been through the training, and were anxious to get the rest of Cosmos' crew qualified. It opened up a significant part of the galaxy, with all its mysteries, just waiting to be known.

Colonel Stahls had worked hard in his qualifying process to overcome some accusations that he was favored because of his family name. His grandfather had reached the Moon at the very beginning of space flight. He, Leslie James Stahls, now had to qualify and fly the corridors of space for himself. Soon, after appointment by NASA and congress, he was endorsed by all around him.

The first time he ordered Cosmos to power up, which was soon after receiving the notice from the Omni-Star concerning the asteroid, he went directly to the stairs and down into the engine room and walked among the rotor pods just to hear them start up and deliver that distinct hum. He patted a few of them fondly. The tech crew and chief were watching. That gesture registered something significant to them. The rotor pods had become known as Dolan's Angels. Chief Dolan, aboard the Omni-Star, Colonel Austin's Engine Room Chief, would be retiring upon their return to Earth from their current mission. His 'angels' would not. There was a galaxy to explore and many young highly qualified explorers standing at the ready.

Chapter 4

R & R

Spaceport Zeta

Colonel Austin and his crew, with Mentar and his team, recovered from the all-night celebration of the rescue of Spaceport Zeta from the near-disaster. In the afternoon, the scientific researchers returned to the library and continued their work.

After a meeting with the Zeta Commander to record the details of the near-death of Zeta into the historical archives, Jimmy and Mentar returned to the library to check on the science team. They were still vigilantly working toward the goal of discovering Earth's and Zannia's beginnings. There was a note waiting at the library desk for Colonel Austin. Cubicle number 17 had information that might be of interest to the commander. It wasn't the desired information the team was searching for, but it seemed significant enough to point it out to the colonel.

Jimmy and his first officer walked the three hundred feet to cubicle 17. The older scientists motioned for the colonel to look at a monitor. After entering a code, on the screen appeared a group of three pyramids. It was as if they were viewing the pyramids of Giza in Egypt. The relative size to each other was the same, and the alignment was the same.

"Is there a Sphinx!?" Jimmy inquired.

"I checked that; not exactly. Take a look at this." He adjusted the monitor to the side of the cluster of pyramids and across about a quarter mile of reddish sand then adjusted the focus.

"A Centaur!" Jimmy exclaimed.

On the screen was a half-horse-half-man sphinx in stone about a hundred feet long and soaring some sixty to eighty feet into the sky.

"Colonel," the researcher said, "these people, if that's what they are, must have been to Earth. And it looks like it was long ago, perhaps thousands of years ago. And, according to the carvings and pictures found in Egypt, they had at least one of these things, these Centaurs, with them, unless, of course, it's a civilization of Centaurs. Those ancient peoples in Egypt must have carved and painted what they saw."

"Or," Jimmy added, "the people of that planet created live centaurs through DNA manipulation of horses, after arriving on Earth to awe the Egyptians, or maybe to control them, to have the Egyptians serve them while they were there... Where is this planet—how far away?"

"Its file-name is Malcore. It's orbiting a red dwarf, AG 3082A. It's 11.4 lightyears from here; about 14 from Earth. It might be a planet we would want to visit."

"No doubt about it," Colonel Austin agreed. "Log all of that information, with images."

"Already done, sir."

Jimmy and Bruce returned to the waiting area, then Jimmy contacted all the scientists' communicators at once. "Gentlemen," he began, "I suggest that the entire team take a break. Mark where you are in your search, then take the rest of today and all day tomorrow off for some rest and relaxation. Get a good meal, take in a show at one of the theaters; they have real Earth popcorn now. Or just kick back and let your mind and body rest. Perhaps it will yield some fresh insight and I know everyone could use a break."

All agreed, and soon, all the transports were occupied and on their way to the Omni-Star for the weary researchers to freshen up and enjoy some R & R. The first couple of hours would be spent communicating with their families on Earth. None could yet answer the first question they were asked. But it would come. It would surely come. After two weeks of searching the records at Zeta's fabled library, their confidence of finding a clue that would lead to an answer, was unshaken.

Jimmy placed a call to Starship Little One. Momentarily, Kronos came online.

"Kronos," Jimmy began, "how goes the journey?"

"I am happy to report that Starship Little One is performing well. You *little ones* of Earth know how to build a ship."

"Good. How's the teacher and the cowboy doing?"

"Fine. Just fine. They're touring the ship, slowly and thoroughly. Brad is curious about everything. The guy has a great mind. He learns fast."

"However," Jimmy interjected, "to leap-frog a couple of centuries would be a challenge for anyone."

Kronos continued, "I offered them suspended animation for the ship time in route. They want to stay awake and soak up, as they put it, this spacefaring experience."

"Give them a couple of months, they may want some sleep time."

"I'll leave the offer open for them. Brad has talked to his grandson a couple of times. When he found out that Jeremy was a rotor pod technician, he went down and toured the engine room. Our staff spent quite a bit of time with him. He says he wants to work with the rotor pods along with his grandson. I told him Zannia could use another tech. So, it's settled; he wants to enter training as an apprentice upon arrival on Zannia."

"I'm glad to hear that," Jimmy said. "He needs his hands tied to something."

Chapter 5

FOUND

Several days later, near a month since the vigil in the spaceport library began, Howard Wiggins, already labeled 'Starman', and his associate, Dole Wheeler, concluded their search in their cubicle and moved to the next unexplored candidate. Settling in, Howard turned on the electronics and selected English. The name of the planet, Concavia, was displayed on the monitor momentarily, then it faded out and a caption, in bold print, spread across the screen:

THE ONLY KNOWN HOLLOW PLANET

Below that caption was the planet's symbol; a depiction of a planet-sized geode with what appeared to be large clouds with streamers connecting to the surface.

Howard turned to his assistant. "Look at this!"

"I see it. How exactly would a hollow planet work?"

"Good question." Howard said, "let's get the basic information recorded." He pressed RECORD on the control panel. The monitor began scrolling information and producing a hard copy. When it finished the basic stats, the equipment went silent. Howard picked up the hard copy and began to read.

"The planet Concavia is 44.5 lightyears from Spaceport Zeta in the mean direction of the galactic core. It orbits Trappist 1, a cooler orange star. Concavia is one of seven planets in that system and is the planet closest to the star. There's a wormhole vortex, 2.1 lightyears from the Trappist 1 system.

"Concavia, terraformed for habitation on the inside over three hundred thousand years ago, has a mean diameter of twelve thousand miles." Howard paused. "Okay, it's a terraformed planet; not natural." He continued.

"Inside gravity strength is an acceleration of 5.25 feet per second squared."

Howard paused again. "The gravity is about the same as Earth's moon. That means, given the diameter of the planet, there's a lot of mass missing from inside. It's not just a large cave in the planet, it's actually a hollow world. What an unusual phenomenon. It has to be the product of a gigantic Supernova; perhaps something in the neighborhood of the star VY Canis Majoris. Majoris is about two billion miles in diameter. A supernova that big might produce a planet sized geode, like Concavia."

"How is the energy from the star transferred inside the planet?" Dole inquired. "Without sunlight, how would a species survive?"

Howard scanned down the page, then turned to the second. "Here it is."

He read. *"Concavia is honeycombed with heat collectors spaced around the planet that transfer the star's heat and light all the way through the 250-mile-*

thick shell to heat the interior. Also, there are electricity generating grids exposed to the sun, also reaching through the mantle.

"Additional heat and light for the interior of the planet come from a sphere, an artificial sun, the Concavians made and placed there early in their occupation of this world. It is 50 miles in diameter and is held at the center of the inner space by the mutually opposing forces of the planet's gravity, created by the centrifugal force of its rotation. While still unknown, it is assumed that the artificial sun is powered by some sort of internal nuclear-fusion generator."

Howard returned to the top of the next page of the document and continued to read:

"Concavia is occupied by a race of humanoids, numbering approximately five hundred million, inside the hollow world. Concavia's labs create different lifeforms by DNA manipulation, then seed barren planets with these lifeforms for research purposes."

"What's going on here?" Howard said. "Are these people...uh, beings, trying to play God. It says they stock barren planets with lifeforms?"

"It seems like it."

Howard was quiet for a few moments. "I'm going to call the colonel; this looks like what we are looking for. They could have been responsible for planting the giants, or whatever became the giants, on Zannia."

In a few minutes, Colonel Austin entered the cubicle. "What have you found?"

"Colonel, according to the writeup, these people seed planets with lifeforms. I'm wondering if they seeded Zannia and then whatever they seeded there became the giants that we discovered on our Moon."

"As far-fetched as that sounds, I suppose it may be possible. However, a trip of 44.5 lightyears is a long way to go, even with the advantage of the wormhole. We will need more evidence than just the fact that they exercise the science of seeding and monitoring. Keep digging until you find some ironclad evidence of a Moai or a similar large statue. Short of that, we cannot commit."

"Yes, sir."

Jimmy turned to Bruce. "I've got a gut feeling they've found it; but we've got to have solid evidence."

"Yes, sir, I agree. Just give them more time. They will nail it down one way or the other."

The team turned back to their task to begin digging for something tangible to ascertain if this would be the correct destination.

"The name of the planet," Dole interrupted, "Concavia. That sounds Italian."

"Yeah, it does," Howard agreed.

"Wait a minute," Dole said, "one of the guys in the European group is Italian. His name is Marian Alonzo. Let's get him in here; I'm curious." Dole pulled out his copy of the roster for the scientists aboard the Omni-Star and entered Marian's personal code in his communicator.

"Marian," he said, "this is Dole Wheeler; would you step over here to cubicle 27 for a moment? I want you to look at something."

Momentarily, the Italian scientist walked in and looked at Dole expectantly. Dole scrolled the monitor back to the beginning, then paused it on the first image, the name of the planet; Concavia. "Is that Italian?"

"Yes," Marian replied promptly. "It means opening, cave, hollow space."

Dole smiled, then moved the monitor to the next image, showing the bold statement:

THE ONLY KNOWN HOLLOW PLANET

"It's a planet?!" Marian said loudly. The scientists in the surrounding cubicles all looked toward 27, then started making their way over to it. "Wait," Marian said. "I want to check something." He located the control and switched the language back to the planet's own language and scanned it momentarily. "This is a form of Italian, very close to ancient Italian formerly spoken on Earth! There are minor differences but they're negligible. That's interesting; perhaps they've been to Earth."

Howard, noticing the group of observers was growing, switched the language back to English, then scanned back to the basic stats for the planet and reviewed them briefly. When the group heard of the seeding activity, suggestions began to flow from the group of scientific minds.

"Go to search, then put in monument,' came from someone in the crowd.

Howard did so, and the monitor scrolled several monuments displayed in several of the planet's cities.

"Try statues." More scenes scrolled across the monitor of towns and their honorariums.

"Wait a minute,' Howard said. "They were doing seeding for research." Howard turned to the keyboard then typed in: **PLANET WITH TWO SUNS**

The monitor went dark for a couple of seconds, then flashed on. Displayed was a Moai in the foreground and in the background, the twin mountains of Zannia's Peak Island, barren, rising above the clouds.

"Bingo!!!" Dole shouted and then heard it echo through the library. Colonel Austin looked in the direction of cubicle 27. A dozen of the scientists were waving their arms, gesturing for the colonel to come to the cubicle. Jimmy hurriedly walked to the group. Howard pointed to the monitor. Jimmy stepped over to it and stared, transfixed, for several seconds.

"Ladies and gentlemen, we know where we came from. Let's journey there together and claim our heritage!"

He turned to Howard, then looked around at the group of scientists. "Get every ounce of information from this cubicle about Concavia. We need to know everything there is to know about this planet. Then we will pay them a visit. Howard," Jimmy continued, "get me the bearing and distance."

Howard brought it up and printed a hard copy. Jimmy looked it over, then up and around at the group. "Great job everybody. Drinks are on me at the Spirits and Song tonight. Now, if you gentlemen will excuse me, I have some phone calls to make."

*After finding the Omni Star earlier, the four-foot-tall humanoid had been shadowing Colonel Austin, being careful to remain incognito. His light frame, oversized hairless head, and smooth grey face helped him blend in with the myriad of species transiting the spaceport. After sneaking into the library, he been watching cubicle 27. The scientists from Earth had entered it and began their search. He had heard other species around the spaceport discussing the quest undertaken by the giants and humans, to find a specific destination having to do with a certain unusual statue, a Moai, they called it. Everyone had heard that the humans and giants would be going to whatever planet they discovered might possibly be their birthplace…their origin. The alien knew it **had** to be his planet. As a citizen of the hollow world, he had not been privy to the details of Concavia's practice of seeding barren planets and moons with experimental DNA. But he **was** guilty of starting a movement to ban the practice. When his group of dissenters began to grow and flourish, the powers-that-be felt threatened, and in a desperate move to eliminate descent, they banished Akela Antonyo from Concavia for life.*

He sought and was granted asylum on Spaceport Zeta. When his exile had begun, and he arrived on

Zeta, he had to go through six months of conditioning therapy to adjust to the gravity of the space station. It was very difficult because of his age, but he survived.

He had been on this distant space station for 26 years now. He had volunteered to mix drinks at the Spirits and Song to fill his days. He wanted to return home and petition the present leadership for mercy to allow him to be with his family in his last years. When the Earth ship arrived, and he learned of their quest, he saw it as a possible a ride home and a chance to be reunited with his own.

He would seek out this commander and petition him to allow him to board his ship and be transported back to Concavia and petition for the chance for renewed life with his family.

Chapter 6

THE CONCAVIAN

The Omni-Star
Main Deck Conference Room

Colonel Austin looked around at his bridge crew, Mentar and his team, ship's security chief, and a smattering of scientists, including Starman, that were asked to attend the impromptu meeting. The colonel reviewed the bearing and distance printout to the planet Concavia again. It read:

CONCAVIA

Compass bearing, 280 degrees. Galactic plane, + 2.3 degrees. Distance, 44.5 lightyears.

Jimmy looked around at the assembled group. "The last couple of hours, I've been on a conference call with NASA, the president, and a congressional liaison. Now that we know where we believe we will find our destiny, things have taken on a serious tone. Due to the maximum stress endured by our crafts recently, it is our collective judgement that we return to Earth, undergo a complete maintenance review of the Omni-Star and all excursion craft, especially the DOEs. Further, when Cosmos returns from her wormhole

71

training flight, she will be reviewed as well and be outfitted to fly with the Omni-Star to the planet Concavia."

The meeting came alive with expressions of agreement and praise for adding another starship and the safety it could provide.

Jimmy continued, "The big concern is the distance from home. With two starships, we double our chances of a safe and productive mission. I also petitioned NASA to do something on these starships that has been on our minds for some time now. I've asked them to equip both ships with artificial gravity. After considerable discussion, in which I had to assure them of the availability of the system from the Zylons, they began preparations for the modifications. The Zylons will be happy to trade two of the systems for a generous amount of Earth's coveted commodity, Neodymium. The availability of magnetic metals on Zylon is very limited.

So, both ships will be so equipped before the journey to Concavia. Now, as soon as our scientists are satisfied with their information gathered on Concavia, we'll be on our way to Earth."

Jimmy asked Howard to petition the library for data copies of the star charts from Spaceport Zeta to Concavia and to download the schematic of the wormhole system. Then he looked around at the group again. "I'll see everybody at Spirits and Song for our victory party tonight!"

With that, Jimmy concluded the meeting, then turned to Mentar and his colleagues. "Mentar, we will be on Earth for a number of months. It will be an opportunity for you to visit with your people at Mentar City."

"We were just discussing that, Colonel. Since you and Earth's leadership have decided to add Cosmos to the quest, we would like to have the colonists elect five representatives of the colony to join us and fly on Cosmos."

"Of course," Jimmy said. "I'll put you in communication with the colony, so you can notify them, and they can begin the selection process. They'll be happy to hear that you are coming to town. Oh, by the way, don't forget your robot down in R & D."

"I talked to them about an hour ago. They've finished all the circuits. They are going to replace his processor. Its speed is far too slow for the programming upgrade. He should be ready tomorrow."

The Spirits and Song Club – late evening.

Seven notified the Spirits and Song club to expect, perhaps a hundred or more guests from the Earth ship at the club for the evening. It would be a large celebration. The androids brought in extra furniture, tables and chairs, to accommodate a packed house. Soon, merriment prevailed, and the atmosphere was electric as the scientists, usually very disciplined and orderly, began to loosen up and enjoy themselves. Awkward toasts were enjoyed several times. The most noted was a toast to Starman for the input about the planet with two suns, and then Doles' echoing *"Bingo."*

Akela Antonyo, the four-foot-tall exile from Concavia, passed the word that he wanted to see Seven. He petitioned the android to give a message to the commander of the starship from Earth. Seven made his way to the colonel's table and leaned down close to him. *"Colonel, do you have a minute?"*

"Yes, Seven, what's going on; what's up?"

"Akela Antonyo would like to talk to you."

"Who's Akela Antonyo." What's this about?"

"Colonel…he's Concavian."

Jimmy froze momentarily, got to his feet, then turned to Seven. "Some of them are here?!"

"Only Akela, and he's been here 26 years."

"Twenty-six years?!"

"Yes, Colonel. He's in exile. He was banished from his planet for life for a political crime. He was granted asylum on Zeta. He has asked to talk to you."

Jimmy sat back down in thought for a few moments, then stood again and signaled to his first officer, Bruce Wilson. Bruce picked up his drink and made his way to the colonel's table.

"Bruce," Jimmy said. "Seven just brought me a message that one Akela Antonyo wants to talk to me. He's from Concavia."

"Really!"

"However, he's been here on Zeta for 26 years, banished from his home world for life. Some political crime."

"Can he be trusted?!"

"I don't know. I want you with me to talk to him. I've got a gut feeling what he wants to talk to me about. Let's go see what he wants," Jimmy concluded and nodded to Seven.

Bruce set his drink down and followed. "We can learn a lot from him."

Seven lead them down a hallway on one side of the club and into an office. Standing in the middle of the room was the four-foot tall Concavian. He looked up at Jimmy, then at Bruce, then back to Jimmy. With his translator in place, he spoke. "Commander, I would like to board your ship and go with you to Concavia."

Jimmy stared for a moment. "Why? I understand that you have been banished from your home world. We cannot interfere with the laws of another planet or influence its government."

"I understand that, sir," Akela responded. "But I want to petition the present leaders of Concavia and beg their mercy that they set aside my conviction and allow me to return to my family in my final years."

Jimmy paused again, looked at Bruce, then back to the Concavian. "What was your crime. It must have been pretty severe to extract such punishment?"

Akela gestured for Colonel Austin and Bruce to sit down at an oblong table. He seated himself and spoke. "Over the many millennia, on Concavia, our society evolved into two distinct groups; the elites, who are the scientists and the government officials, and the citizens, those of us who just live out our lives and raise our families. When we learned about the extensive nature of our elites manipulating the DNA of other worlds, without regard to their lives, a few of us organized a protest to get them to reconsider their meddling in other planet's natural evolution. Somehow, it just seemed wrong.

"Since my name was on the protest information passed around, they assumed I was the organizer, although I was only one of five planners of the protest. It was the first time in our history that a common citizen had challenged the government's decisions. They perceived my political activity as an attempt to overthrow the government.

"Now, all I want is a chance to return to my family. Some have asked me why I don't communicate with my planet and petition them via Quantum Communications. I want to make my appeal in person. I want to have a real chance."

Colonel Austin was quiet for a moment. "I can identify with that. I also want to make our request of those leaders in person. I want to look them in the eye."

Jimmy's first officer spoke directly to the Concavian. "And if the leaders refuse to grant you access back to the planet, what then?"

"Then, I will petition Earth to grant me Asylum."

Jimmy looked up. "Okay, I'm satisfied. But don't pack your bags yet. I will talk with Earth's leaders and let you know."

"*He's already packed, Colonel,*" Seven said.

Jimmy glanced from Seven back to the Concavian. He smiled disarmingly. Jimmy smiled back, "Okay, I will check this out and let you know our decision. Seven will be in touch with you."

Jimmy and Bruce returned to the party. Jimmy leaned close to Bruce. "Let's not mention that there's a Concavian here and that we're considering letting him join us aboard ship until I have a chance to confer with NASA and the president."

"Understood, sir. They would be all over him wanting to know about the planet."

"Yeah, they would. And I don't think Akela knows the answers we seek. He seems to be an ordinary citizen that just voices his and his friends' opinions about government activity."

"I agree," Bruce said. "He probably had no idea how seriously the government would take the issue. It looks like the group just began to demonstrate against government action. Sounds familiar doesn't it?"

The festivities at the Spirits and Song went on well into the night. Jimmy was glad to see the merriment and to hear the richness of victory in the voices of the scientists. They had worked hard in the effort to find the elusive world thought to be mankind's and the giant's true origin.

A group of the scientists spent two more days in cubicle 27. Among the general information they logged, they discovered that in the planet's history, it had been occupied and abandoned three times. Then, a technologically advanced civilization found it, terraformed the inside surface of the planet to their liking, named it Concavia, and became its permanent residents. They had wanted an out-of-the-way planet because of the controversy their seeding activities had created in parts of the galaxy. Details were sketchy and the mystery was tantalizing.

Mentar got a call from R & D that Zolaadine Man was ready. He asked Jimmy to accompany him to pick up his personal robot. Prior to replacing his processor and his data storage banks, R & D made a copy of his previous data files for Mentar.

He had been named Zoll by his creators, for an obvious reason. He was constructed of zolaadine just at the beginning of the construction of Zannia 2, the huge starship the giants built to abandon Zannia when it became inhabitable. Zoll's job had been to pilot the vertical transport up and down the space elevator ferrying parts, tools, and supplies to Zannia 2 during its construction in the atmosphere. It was a great savings of time and effort, since no oxygen or pressure was needed for a robot.

Zoll's data base did not reveal how he was damaged by the industrial laser. It had come from behind him and simultaneously wiped out his conscience circuits. It was likely that the incident happened at or near the launch of Zannia 2. Rather than take along a damaged robot, Zoll was placed in the field away from the launch area where he had been found.

Now, he was as serviceable as Seven, having updated equipment and programming. He would be

Mentar's right hand man…or assistant. It was a timely assignment, considering Mentar's age. Analyzing Zoll before the upgrade, Jimmy had placed his sophistication about halfway between the old TV series character, Robbie the Robot, and the modern android, Seven. Now, with his processor and programming upgrade, he could pass as Seven's little brother, with near-full android capabilities. Mentar would find him useful and good company.

The Omni-Star and crew were ready to set sail for Earth. They looked forward to some crew R&R and a maintenance review of the ship before embarking on the journey to Concavia. Colonel Austin called the crew together for a ship-wide conference. Those on essential crew duties and others not inside the conference room were in attendance vis video feeds. Jimmy went to the podium, then addressed the crew:

"First, I want to say again that everybody did a great job here at Spaceport Zeta. We now have the information we need to seek out the answer to what we've all been wondering about. Also, you should know that I have been informed that there's a Concavian here in the Spaceport."

The floor exploded with gasps and murmurings. Jimmy held up his hand. Gradually the hall became quiet. The colonel continued. "He's been here 26 years; he's an exile, in asylum here at the spaceport. His name is Akela Antonyo. Seven arranged for Bruce and I to talk with him three days ago. He told us that he was banished from Concavia for a political crime that the leaders deemed to be grave. He had started a political movement to stop the government from seeding planets and moons with various forms of DNA and then doing follow up studies. The planet's leaders took his actions as an attempt to overthrow the government and banished him from Concavia. He requested and received asylum here on Zeta. He has not been on his planet for 26 years. We all know how much change can take place in almost three decades.

"He has asked for Asylum on Earth, and then wants to go with us to Concavia and petition the present leaders of the planet's government to exercise mercy and set aside his conviction and allow him to rejoin his family in his final years."

"Well, let's take him home!" some shouted from the crowd.

Jimmy continued. "I contacted Earth. NASA, the President, and a congressional liaison headed up by someone who knows about exile; Senator Stahls, agreed to grant him asylum on Earth. And he will be going with us to Concavia. Now, he's not part of the government nor the scientific community of Concavia and would not know the answers we seek about our origins. So, let's not quiz him to death. Bruce, please go and tell Akela that his asylum has been approved."

"Sir, the head of security just told me he's standing at the end of the ramp with two suitcases."

There was chuckling among the crew. Jimmy smiled. "Okay, go ahead and bring him aboard and assign him quarters. Uh, bring him here to the hall first so everybody can meet him."

"Yes, sir."

Bruce nodded and the head of security turned away, put his communicator close to his mouth, and spoke into it.

Main deck security officers, George Manly, 48, and Steven Copeland, 26, stepped off the end of the ramp, picked up Akela's two suitcases, then gestured toward the ramp. "You're in," George said.

Akela, stuck both arms straight up and uttered a two-word phrase that only he and the two nearby androids, understood. The four-foot tall Concavian, entering the ship with the security guards, was taking almost two steps to one of his escorts. At the top of the ramp, they stepped onto the expansive floor of the main deck of the Omni-Star.

Across the way, the door of Ship's Records opened and Dedra Allison, 4'10", came out, carrying her electronic recording pad. She headed for the bridge to check the readouts as she did twice daily during her shift. She saw Akela walking toward her between the two security guards. She smiled at him. He smiled back. She continued on her task. His gaze followed her as she walked away. He inadvertently walked into Steven, and then the guard on his right, and then stumbled and was about to fall. George, the guard on his left, caught him and put him back on his feet. He then looked toward the record's specialist as she continued toward the bridge.

"They made some sort of connection," George commented.

Steven smiled. "We'll keep an eye on him."

Akela looked up from one guard to the other, then at the floor. They smiled at him and gestured toward the conference hall. When they stepped through the doorway, there were murmurings through the crowd, then applause began as the Concavian approached the Colonel with his two escorting guards one step behind him, still carrying his suitcases. He turned toward the applauding crew and extended both arms straight up in a victory gesture, smiling broadly.

"He's a political type, that's for sure," Colonel Austin said to no one in particular, then joined in the applause.

Within hours, Akala was on the first leg of his journey home.

Kuiper Belt – The Solar System

During the three months' travel time, from the wormhole vortex to Earth, during one of Jimmy and Mentar's daily briefings, Mentar looked at Jimmy with a thoughtful expression.

"Colonel, my friend, I have made a decision."

Jimmy, turned, suspecting what his friend was about to say.

Mentar, after a moment's hesitation, said, "I have decided that when we return from Concavia, I will retire on Earth."

Jimmy smiled. "My friend, I will be pleased to have you as a fellow Earthling. With your permission I will notify the President of your decision."

Mentar nodded. "By then Menvaar will be in his third year of Starship Training. I will have the opportunity to spend more time with him than I have in recent years. My duties on Zannia were somewhat demanding."

Jimmy smiled and placed his hand on the giant's massive arm. "I understand. A father and son need to nurture the bond intended for them. I'm sure he will appreciate your encouragement during training."

During the trip home from Zeta, Marian Alonzo, the Italian translator, was the most popular soul on board, second only to Akela. The automatic translators had been left behind, since they belonged to Zeta. NASA's technicians were already working on a similar device for crews of Earth's fleet.

On board the ship, Marian had translated for the multiple meetings of the ship's crew with the Concavian. The last week of the flight, Colonel Austin isolated Akela to allow him to rest up for the same flurry that was sure to come when they touched down on Earth. One of the first persons he was scheduled to meet officially was Senator Roger Stahls. Akela had been told the story of Roger's abandonment and his time in suspended animation along with the giants, in tunnels underneath the Moon. He was very excited at the coming meeting.

When the Omni-Star closed on Earth, Akela was standing at the ship's windshield, staring at the blue and white world. He whispered one of the few words he had made a point to learn in English. *"Beautiful."* It was the first planet he'd seen in 26 years.

Chapter 7

ARRIVAL

The Omni-Star settled onto the tarmac at the Frank Gordon Space Flight Center amid a massive welcome, led by the President, the NASA Director, the aged Senator Roger Stahls, and the Director of the Museum of Natural History. Worldwide news outlets had sent crews to give their countries a first glance of the *'little grey alien,'* as he had become known. All wanted to see the representation of the destination planet, possibly harboring the answer to mankind's greatest question.

The President welcomed the Omni Star's crew and congratulated them on their research skills, which had set the stage for the upcoming mission to Concavia. He then turned and motioned for Akela to step forward. Marian Alonzo accompanied him to translate. The applause was deafening. Much to the delight of the crowd and the media outlets Akela raised his hand and waved like a politician. When the President moved from the podium, a technician placed a raised platform there for Akela. He stepped up to the mic and said in halting English, "T h a n k   y o u   f o r   y o u r   h o s   p o- t a l i t y."

The applause was long and loud. Marian translated for Akela's additional remarks. He thanked Colonel Austin for giving him a ride home and expressed Austin for the ride home and expressed gratitude to the President for welcoming him and offering a permanent future home on Earth for him and his family if needed. He expressed hope for being accepted back on Concavia.

Following his speech, the photo-ops and handshakes with the dignitaries would fill news-cycles for the coming weeks.

After removal of the small platform, the President stepped back to the podium. He motioned for Mentar to join him and then he announced that Mentar had decided to retire atter the coming mission and that he had selected Earth as his retirement home. The giants in attendance from their Earth Colony raised their arms in a salute to Mentar for his decision. He responded with the same salute to them. After the applause had died down, the President announced that the government wanted to honor him and his contribution to both Zannia and Earth.

He then introduced the Director of the Museum of Natural history to make a special presentation. The Director took the podium. "Welcome home, especially to you, Mentar. We are all pleased that you have chosen to retire on Earth. In honor of your contribution to Earth, we have a special gift for you. Recently, during NASA's sonic mapping of the Alps, they discovered yet another Moai statue partially buried in a remote forest area. Nearby, there were some remains of an ancient site of unknown origin. Archeologists believe it predates the oldest remains previously found on Earth. NASA commissioned teams from several nations to investigate but none could identify the ruins. The possibility of alien involvement in the site is being investigated. They even searched for the evidence of any comrades of your who may have at the site at some time in the past, but none were found. We retrieved the statue and stored it here. We now present it to you as a retirement gift. Please follow us into the hangar."

The entire crowd, including the crew and their families, moved to inside the hangar. The giant gleaming black Moai was on display, spot-lighted from several angles. Mentar, Akela, Jimmy and the Museum director walked past the crowd barrier and then around the giant statue first, noting that it was in pristine condition. The rest of the crew and the families who had been waiting were still greeting each other and soon joined in the viewing of the Moai.

The Museum Director, followed by the President, walked up to the soon to retire giant. "Mentar, we will erect this statue at the place of your choosing as a testimonial to your contributions to our mutual space efforts."

Mentar commented. "Mr. Director, I am impressed...thank you. I notice that this Moai is hewn more exactly than the one in Mentar City and is in pristine condition. This has to have been designed for a special purpose...it must be displayed in a special place. I request that you display it here at the Frank Gordon Space Flight Center to forever salute those who enter here and reach for the stars."

The Director, with a nod from the President, looked up at Mentar. "I'll make the arrangements."

Following the ceremony for Mentar, the scientists and astronomy graduates made their way back to their home countries to meet with colleagues and to tour and speak for the next few months. In their belongings were many treasures to share with those who had waited on Earth. The crew and their families departed for some needed 'home-time' and family reunions.

When the graduate astronomer, Amil Lajahda, arrived in his hometown, his mother and father, an aging missionary, and representatives from his university were waiting. He embraced everyone, then hugged his mother several times. He reached into his bag and came out with the Starlite, virtually weightless, oval-shaped gift from Meta, the blue-skinned female from planet Lindia. His mother stared at it. Amil placed it in her hand. "That came from inside a star. The star exploded and that landed on a moon. This girl I met gave it to me. Her father found it on a small moon in their star system."

"Girl?" his mother said with a smile.

Amil picked up his communicator and brought up the image he had taken of her at the spaceport during lunch, then showed it to his mother. She stared at the Lindian's bluish skin, her larger crystal-clear blue eyes, and with smile on her face, she looked up at Amil and spoke in Hindi.

Amil translated. "Star Princess? No, Mother. She's a technician. She was studying in the library like I was. We had lunch together."

He could tell that his mother was not hearing the alternative explanation. She nodded with a knowing smile and held the crystal-clear oval to her breast. Amil looked around at the others in their party, then hugged his mother again. Amil's father looked at the image on the communicator and smiled and nodded. He passed it around to their friends and associates, speaking to them in Hindi.

The Omni-Star was moved to the maintenance pad for a complete shakedown. Colonel Austin was notified that arrangements had been made with the Zylons. They were due in ten days and would arrive in two ships. One, with the gravity generating systems and the technicians to do the installation, and another cargo ship to be loaded with 50 tons of Neodymium from Earth's reserves. Interplanetary trade at its finest.

Colonel Austin ordered that one of the guppies from each starship be outfitted with six seats, giant size, and six seats, *little-one*-size, to be used for ship-to-ship meetings and mutual transportation during the mission.

An Air Force liaison contacted Captains Snyder and Abbott. The Air Force was replacing the two DOEs with new ones, as the old ones had been flying for many years and one of them had suffered some damage doing its duty to help stop the Zeta near-disaster. Both crews were interviewed by their superiors and Air Force medical, to determine if they wanted to step down and accept retirement. Following an intense physical, they were deemed physically fit and qualified to complete the upcoming mission. Both chose unanimously to continue on, explaining that they had come this far and so wanted to know the answer being sought by the crew of the Omni-Star. Approved to continue, the captains and crews saluted the retired DOEs as they flew away into the distance. They were good ships and would continue to be used inside the solar system. Then, they turned their eyes to the new ones. They noticed on the words etched into the frame of the machines, **Property of the Omni-Star**. They boarded them, and immediately then took them out for a shakedown. Maybe the old saying was true; *"Pilots had rather fly than eat."*

The other ships on board the Omni Star, the two Quads, the high-powered versions of the guppies, were checked for readiness although they had yet to log a single hour of space flight time. They had already traversed many lightyears in their hangar bay, silently awaiting a need, each standing by with a beefed-up guppy frame and 4 rotor pods of power.

The Omni-Star knew her next destination, the possible 'cradle of life,' whatever it may turn out to be, was Concavia. It was an Italian name. Many tried to connect some significance to the fact that the language at destination was almost identical to ancient Italian, spoken earlier on Earth. Many wondered if the

Concavians had been to Earth and, perhaps, seeded some of early man? But there was not yet any solid evidence of such an occurrence.

Jimmy knew that in the late 1900s, the first giants had been discovered in suspended animation, in caves on Earth's moon. He and Mentar had discussed it many times. Those who explored the giants' extensive laboratories on the Moon had discovered what appeared to be experiments with early humans and apes. Scientists were now wondering if the Concavians might have had a hand in setting humanity in motion. They and Jimmy all agreed that the answer would only come when standing face to face with Concavian scientists.

There were a lot of questions on this mission. Thanks to Quantum Communications, Earth would not have to wait five or ten years to know some of the answers. What was to be learned could be communicated to Earth as it is learned; positive or not. The crew would petition for the plain truth. It would be forthcoming. The commander stated unequivocally that he would not fly a dangerous long-distance mission to transmit a bunch of fluff back home. It would be the truth, the plain truth, whatever it is.

Spirits and Song Club
Wichita, Kansas

Jimmy, the Omni Star Bridge Crew and the giant contingent entered the Earth version of the Spirits and

Song Club, located just outside the spaceflight center complex. A group of entrepreneurs, knowing its popularity at Spaceport Zeta, got together and duplicated the club layout with the 'two-sized' furniture and fixtures, for both giants and *little ones*. They petitioned and received the menu offerings of the original club on Zeta, up to and including the 'smoke beads' dropped into the drinks for effect. Upon the return of the Omni-Star, and learning that Akela had been mixing drinks on Zeta for years, they petitioned the Concavian to give a seminar behind the bar. He complied and made Earth's Spirits and Song, 'official.'

"How about this place," Jimmy said. "I like this!"

"Our planets are starting to mesh," Bruce agreed. "Before you know it, Zeta will have a McDonalds with veggie burgers and smoking fruit drinks."

Laughter spread through the group, including the noticeable low-pitched chuckles from the Zannians. The group settled down around the special-made tables and began relaxing. The manager, notified that the starship's crew was there, came out and personally welcomed them and ordered that the first round of drinks be on-the-house. The drinks were served, columns of smoke and all, and the party was underway. The band, "The Moonies," had been signed on by the Spirits and Song to provide the music for the club. They now had a regular billing.

Idle conversation filled the establishment as the evening wore on. Many adventures relived and smiled upon as the seasoned crew talked among themselves.

Then, a member of the medical staff at Mentar City, entered the Spirits and Song and sought out Mentar. He stepped to his side and spoke to him quietly. Jimmy noticed and waited expectantly. Mentar's eyes went down to the table for a long moment, then he turned to Jimmy. "Kaabar passed away in his sleep last night."

Jimmy was quiet for a moment. "Mentar, he lived well beyond his expected years."

"Yes, he did. We challenged him, and he rose to the occasion. He spent his final years contributing to his community. I'm glad."

"Me, too." Jimmy whispered.

The bridge crew, sensing an issue, focused on Colonel Austin. He responded. "Kaabar, the one who helped us retrieve Mentar's lost shuttle at the spaceport, died in his sleep last night."

The bridge crew looked at each other quietly. Finally, Sheldon spoke: "Colonel, we want to go to the Giants' Memorial Service when he's taken to the Moon and laid to rest."

Seeing Mentar's nod, Jimmy agreed.

Kaabar's body was prepped, placed in one of the animation units, sealed in, and placed aboard a guppy. Twelve people from Mentar City were aboard two shuttles. Mentar and his selected team were aboard his shuttle. Jimmy, his bridge crew, and Dwight Cummins, the President's liaison, were aboard the Colonel Austin's personal shuttle. Dwight was delighted to be a part of the ceremony with the giants he had come to respect deeply. Although he was offered a spacesuit, he wished to remain aboard the shuttle with the two designees, the pilot and navigator, and experience the event through the windshield. He was well known to the giants and they were pleased to have his presence at Kaabar's final tribute.

The armada set sail for the Moon and Kaabar's chosen burial place, the memorial chamber with his grandson.

Kaabar's name was added to the Marker; etched in stone, preserved forever on the Moon.

Chapter 8

THE WORLD TOUR

During the Maintenance Stand-down for both ships, the crews engaged in refresher training and trained the new personnel NASA had assigned to be on the upcoming mission. It was also a time for shore leave with families and friends of the crews.

Although Brad Givens, the cowboy rescued in space, had elected to reside on Zannia with his granddaughter and her son, his story was dominate for a period of time, on every television channel. He was honored by the National Cowboy Museum in Oklahoma City by being inducted into their Hall of Fame. The Museum Director coordinated a quantum video link to the Starship Little One, still in route to Zannia from the Zeta Spaceport. The out-of-century cowboy felt very awkward, being interviewed on camera from billions of miles away. His video story would be available for viewing by museum goers for decades to come.

NASA, always concerned with putting their best PR foot forward, coordinated a World Tour for the most famous alien ever to visit Earth—Akela. The giants had been famous for over a half-century. Now, Akela was fresh news. The Space Agency commissioned Colonel Austin and Dedra Allison to accompany Akela and introduce him to the world. Most of the world's major cities were on the itinerary. It would be a whirlwind tour, beginning in Washington, D.C., followed by San Francisco, Kuala Lumpur, Tokyo, Peking, Moscow, London, Berlin and finally, Rome.

Jimmy would address each crowd and give them an overview of their missions to date. He had struggled a little with his speech, finding it easier to address his crew than to stand before a group of dignitaries.

Dedra was chosen to introduce Akela, since she had spent the most time with him, honing his English skills. He was nervous and dreaded speaking his halting brand of the language to such important people. He was looking forward to the last stop in Rome, where he would be in his language element.

Arriving in Washington, they were escorted into the Halls of Congress to address the President, NASA officials, all U.S. law makers and over five billion others, via television. A quantum video link had been established to Starship Little One and to the planet Zannia so that the giant population and the Earth Colony...*Little One City*, could be included.

After the President's ceremonial entry into the chambers, the Speaker of the House introduced him, and he addressed the watching world.

"Ladies and gentlemen, and our giant friends billions of miles away, it has been an incredible number of years, since a small band of brave explorers returned to the Moon late last century. They were in search of the unknown that had been revealed to them in a drawer full of old grainy NASA photos taken during the Apollo space program. As we all know, their discovery of giant humanoids asleep in tunnels underneath the Moon changed our perception of the past and our gaze into the future in ways we could not have imagined. In those few short years we have gone from an uninformed, even ignorant, species to one now aware of an untold number of others in this amazing universe. We have been welcomed and befriended by beings of all kinds from the far reaches of the Milky Way Galaxy. We have been the benefactors of far advanced technology that would have taken eons for us to develop on our own.

"Of course, our greatest asset, the one that has solidified our place in the galactic community, has been the brave crews of our space fleet. Past and present starship commanders and their crews have opened doors to places that we previously just read about in science fiction novels. Equipment and technology are essential, but without the wit, wisdom, and bravery of that original crew those number of years ago, and current starship commanders, like Colonel Jimmy Austin, I'm afraid we would still be gazing upward, just wondering what is out there. Now, he and the brave crews of our two newest starships are about to embark on what will surely be the ultimate mission. I will let him explain." He turned to the seats behind him. "Colonel Austin, welcome home."

The President stepped back and motioned Jimmy toward the podium. Awed by this special moment, Jimmy nervously stood and stepped forward to a standing ovation.

When the audience was finally seated, Jimmy began. "Mr. President and members of this great body, thank you for the rousing welcome. I also want to say hello and welcome to my friends and colleagues on the planet Zannia and on board the Starship Little One, somewhere in space between Spaceport Zeta and Zannia. We are all part of a brotherhood that few will ever fully understand. I'm not sure that even I have grasped the special bond we enjoy.

"It should be obvious to all that we who are privileged to represent Earth in what has become a neighborhood of planets, are doing so because of those who came before. We stand on shoulders that opened the universe to us with technology that has now become primitive. While my crew, and others before, have overcome many emergencies, we could have never been successful without those brave souls. So, please join me in thanking the memory of Douglas Hastings, Dave Henson, Frank Gordon, Isaac Henson, Daniel Stubblefield, Colonel Marvin Andrews and the astronaut who had been left behind on the Moon, who is currently a U.S. Senator, Lieutenant Colonel Roger Stahls."

The entire chamber stood in applause and turned toward the seat occupied by the aging Senator. He also haltingly stood and waved to the crowd.

After a minute or so, Jimmy was able to continue. "In a few short decades since Colonel Stahls was rescued from the Moon, we and our biological brothers, the giants of Zannia, have been to the stars and beyond. Earth and Zannia have entered the

Federation of planets and answered one of man's early questions; *are we alone in the universe?* Obviously, we are not. Now we are only weeks away from launching a mission to seek the answer to the other question; *where did we come from?* Scientists have their own answer, as do theologians from around the world. But mankind, as a whole, seeks a more detailed answer. That is why we of Earth and the giants of Zannia will journey to the planet Concavia.

"As you are aware by now, before leaving the Spaceport Zeta. We met a Concavian who will accompany us to his home planet and give us some insight as to how to approach their leadership with our question. I will let Dedra Allison, who maintains the archives on board the Omni-Star, introduce our esteemed passenger."

Dedra stood to approach the podium. An attendant hurriedly set a stool one foot tall in front of it for her. There was some chuckling in the audience. Dedra looked across the august body, smiled, then walked over and stepped upon the stool. The applause lasted a full minute. She began.

"Thank you, Colonel Austin. Mr. President, ladies and gentlemen and my far-away fellow space travelers, I am humbled to be in the company of Colonel Austin, my commander, and in the presence of this distinguished chamber of government officials. I am grateful for all of you...after all, you approve the money, so I can have the best job in the universe."

The lawmakers and the President laughed in appreciation of that moment of levity. Dedra continued.

"The Concavian we met at the spaceport is Akela Antonyo. He and I became friends because he is the only one on the ship that is shorter than me." More laughter. "Akela had been exiled on Spaceport Zeta for 26 years for defying Concavia's practice of experimenting with DNA manipulation indiscriminately on other planets. We will be returning him to his planet, so he can petition the leaders for clemency and return to his family. As you already know, the President has granted asylum to Akela if his planet still rejects him. Thank you, Mr. President."

Those in the chamber stood and applauded.

"So, without further delay, I introduce to you, Mr. Akela Antonyo."

Akela arose and approached the podium to the rousing applause of the body of lawmakers. He paused a moment, then stepped upon the stool. When the applause finally died, he began.

"Thank you Dedra, Colonel Austin, and you, Mr. President. First, I am sorry for my English is not perfect. But I have already heard my fellow space travelers speak the English more different than many of you. Dedra teach me that Americans in your south parts can be confused by the speaking of those in the north parts." There were a few laughs and some cheers from the lawmakers representing the southern states.

"Concavia is more big than Earth and we all speak same language with same dialect. But I like the difference I see on Earth. Different colors, shapes, sizes and jobs of your species are interesting, but a little confusing. I do not understand your species called 'yankee.'"

Those in the chamber representing the northern U.S. stood, clapped and cheered. Akela was beginning to relax and enjoy his notoriety.

"Thirty years ago, many on Concavia did not think it was good for the scientists to put DNA samples on other planets, just to see what would grow there. It was not good to play like a creator with other species just to make experiments.

"The citizens of my planet did not like it, but most were afraid to say it. So, me and some others went to the government to say it was not right to do that and they should stop. The leaders said we did not know science and for us to go away and let them work. So, we started to do...uh...I think you call them *protests*. Groups would get together in villages and in the capital and wave signs that what they were doing was wrong. The government got mad at us and tried to make us stop.

"We didn't stop, so when they saw me in front of the crowd, they arrested me and said I was the cause of the protest. They said I was guilty of trying to overthrow the government. That was not true but they wanted to make an example to warn others, so they punished my by making me leave my planet, my home and stay away forever. I was a very sad day for me and my family. I asked to live at Spaceport Zeta and I have been there 26 years, as you measure them on Earth."

Akela took a drink of the water provided for him on the podium, and then continued. "I am happy to hear that on Earth you allow peaceful protests. If I am allowed back on my planet, I will tell them about your concept.

"As I traveled space with Commander Austin, and the big one, Mentar, and the Omni Star crew, especially, the one my size...Dedra," she blushed, "I see that you humans and giants on Earth are a special species, living on this special planet. Other species at Zeta talk of you and all you have done in not so many years. All are watching to see your future. I am grateful you welcome me on your planet. I am happy to see your world tomorrow and the many special things here.

"I want to go home and be with my family. But, if it is alright with you, when I can find a way in the future, I will bring my family to Earth for a visit. Thank you all very much."

As Akela raised his hand in a farewell wave, the chamber exploded in applause and cheers. Dedra stepped forward to congratulate him. Colonel Austin joined them. The President shook his hand and posed for a media photo-op. It took over an hour to shake all the hands and recover from the pats on the back. Finally, near midnight, exhausted, he and Dedra and Jimmy rested overnight in the Ritz-Carlton, before beginning their world tour.

British Airways Flight 2317, Berlin to Rome
A wingless Boeing 1277 Aircraft with 821 on board

Akela had enjoyed speaking and experiencing the cities on the World Tour NASA had arranged. But the schedule was wearing on him and he was looking forward to completing the tour in Rome and getting back to the USA. One positive of some many speeches and meetings was the vast improvement in his rendering of English. Now, he was about to be in a place that would understand his language, although it was the more ancient version.

As the flight descended into that ancient city, he was staring out his First-Class window at the countryside. He turned. "This conveyance is still strange to me. It is not as large as your starship, but it is huge, compared to the size of our inner-planet shuttles. And the engine technology... what do you call it?"

Jimmy leaned across the aisle. "Magnetic Inertial Propulsion. It is essentially the same technology as what drives the Omni-Star."

Akela nodded. "Ah, yes, rotor pods—amazing. I am still surprised that you humans only invented them in the last seventy Earth years. The engineers on Concavia will be delighted when they study this; that such simplicity could produce such dependable power."

Jimmy agreed. "Well, honestly, I still don't fully understand it. I'm just glad it works."

To keep the media buzz from disrupting the other passengers, the three of them we asked to deplane last. As they walked out, the familiar cameras and microphones were thrust at them. Akela had been through this, seven times already, but still felt uncomfortable as the focus of attention. He saw a small group to his left, representing what he had seen at the last three stops. Their sign read: CONCAVIAN FAN CLUB. There was a roughly drawn caricature of Akela, looking more like a Roswell, New Mexico alien from the 1940s. He just smiled and waved to them.

After meeting the Mayor of Rome for a photo-op, the group was escorted to waiting limousines outside the terminal.

The next day, at noon, the large stadium was packed with hardly an empty seat. With the preliminary speeches complete, Akela took the podium to rousing applause.

After his speech, in Italian, they were whisked away for a tour of historical Rome, guided by the Italian Director of Antiquities. Akela appreciated the significance of Rome to the humans, since Concavia had a history dating back hundreds of thousands of years.

While the group was exiting the catacombs underneath Rome, the Director mentioned to Akela that he had been on the research team that witnessed the recovery of the most recent Moai, discovered in the Alps. He said, "I found the inscription on the back of the statue to be most interesting."

Akala stopped. "What do you mean. What was the inscription?"

The Director said, "There were two circles, one inside the other. Above were what appeared to be oval-shaped clouds connected to the circles by lines...or maybe streamers. What does that symbol mean?"

Akela looked down in thought, and then back at the Director. "Can you draw what you saw?"

The Director turned to his assistant, who handed him a notebook and pen. He then drew a crude depiction of what he had seen and showed it to him.

Akela studied the drawing and then looked at Jimmy. "I need to see that statue again and look at in more detail."

Jimmy said, "It will be erected by the time we return."

Frank Gordon Space Center

Arriving near midnight, Akela and the tour group went immediately to view the Moai, already installed at the entrance to the Space Flight Center. Tourists had gone for the day and no one was around. The statue was well-lit. Akela went straight to the back of the Moai and found the symbol etched into the stone, about four feet from the bottom. He reached out and touched it, then traced the lines with his fingers. "Colonel, this is the symbol for Concavia. This marking is on all the pattern statues in the science pavilion on our planet. We must return this statue to Concavia. I don't know how it got here, in the mountains of Earth, but it belongs to Concavia. Perhaps they can tell us. We must return it."

Colonel Austin stared at Akela for a long moment. There was something in them; something significant. "I will make the arrangements. Mentar will be going with us; he will endorse it. This statue is more significant than just as a representation of the giants."

Chapter 9

THE CALLING CARD

The Starship Cosmos had passed wormhole training with flying colors. Commander Stahls was proud of his crew and he had gained greater confidence as their Captain. They arrived at the spaceport shortly after the Omni Star had departed for Earth. During their short stay at Spaceport Zeta, they were treated with the respect that the Omni Star had earned by saving Zeta from destruction. Crews from other planets insisted on buying them drinks and sharing many variations of the story of the brave crew of the Omni Star, plowing their way through comet debris to save the way station.

Some planets had already contacted the engineers on Zannia to commission for Waddle Cones to be built for their ships. Zannia's off-planet business would soon be booming.

Finally, Cosmos bade farewell to Zeta and headed home. Their return triggered a flurry of activity. After a short shore leave, the crew engaged in the final preparations for the quest of sailing to Concavia and whatever discovery awaited. With Omni Star having completed its final maintenance review inside the massive hangar, Cosmos took its place inside the only structure that could dwarf the size of the star ships.

The Zylons, having arrived to complete their trade-barter deal, had their construction androids descend on Cosmos and install the artificial gravity system. They turn-keyed its installation in short order. The particulars had been practiced earlier on the Omni-Star. One aspect of the system that Colonel Austin endorsed was that it was designed to stay ON during any flight of the ship. Since a starship encounters varying strengths of gravity fields and varying amounts of acceleration, the system would constantly read the gravity field inside the ship and keep it adjusted to Earth's gravity value. When on Earth and parked, the unit would automatically go to zero. If on the Moon, it would add 5/6^{ths} gravity, producing the equivalent of Earth's gravity field, etc.

With both ships in order and ready for the quest, Jimmy wished the Zylon commander, Summar, and his crew farewell. Summar responded again with "*Journey Mercies.*" Jimmy smiled and nodded to his Zylon friend from the planet circling Bernard's Star. Then, following the diplomatic lip-service and dues, government to government, the Zylons, with their treasure of Neodymium, the base material for the most powerful magnets known in the Universe, departed for home.

On many previous missions, most ships in the fleet had flown close formation while in open space. The question of formation flying while in a wormhole had come to the forefront of discussion. The issue had not been part of Wormhole Training since formation flying was a foreign concept to other species. A call to Zeta and a conversation with the Chief of Training, revealed the requirement to fly single file inside a wormhole. He said that the wormhole system was a 'two-way-street.' There was room inside for formation flying but the risk of collision with another oncoming ship would be greater while in formation. It was a danger the mission did not need.

Timothy Dolan, preparing to retire, was asked to be part of the mission preparation, based on his vast maintenance and space experience. He saw no unusual issues associated with using the rotor pods at any power level while inside a wormhole, since they would be protected from the matter that made up the wormhole. However, he did ask whether the Waddle Cone could be used inside a wormhole. The question had never been asked before because there was no record of random debris inside the wormhole system.

At Mentar's suggestion, Jimmy and Leslie called the lab at the spaceport on Zannia. The scientists who created the Waddell Cone explained in detail. They reminded the captains that ships had no need to engage the Waddell Cone inside the solar system because of the reduced speeds while approaching a destination planet. Therefore, normal formation flying would provide the proper clearance.

Jimmy told them that in their upcoming journey the leg from the final vortex to Trappest 1 would only be two lightyears distance, about a year's flying time. Therefore, they didn't intend to engage the Waddell Cone. It wouldn't make sense to isolate their ships, especially that far from home, when the difference in arrival time would be less than twenty percent, roughly two months. Jimmy and Leslie had already agreed with that procedure. On that final leg, due to their size, the Omni-Star and Cosmos would fly a half-mile apart and would be able, during the trip, to visit ship to ship via shuttles.

After much discussion and analysis among the engineers, they agreed that the Waddle Cone *could* be engaged inside a wormhole. However, to maintain safety with other possible passing ships and to ensure the Cone didn't interfere with the wormhole structure, it should not be used above fifty percent power.

So, the details were set...in the wormhole they would fly single file, using the Waddle Cone only if absolutely necessary, and then at less than fifty percent. They would regroup at each vortex on the route and briefly explore what was there. There were three known vortexes on the chosen route. The last of the three would be at the Trappest 1 Vortex. Then they would fly formation on the final leg to Concavia. The procedures were understood, and final preparations were made as launch day approached.

Colonel Austin stepped toward the podium in front of the 1,863 souls that would be boarding the Omni-Star and Cosmos to fly into history. The 'get-acquainted' meeting was arranged by the two starship commanders, so that all aboard would know who they were flying with. The atmosphere was electric, yet solemn. Some were anxious about what might lie ahead. However, an overwhelming majority were anxious to dig in and find out.

As the conference hall gradually became quiet, the colonel began, "Every warm wiggling soul on this mission, from the hydroponic attendee that waters the tomatoes and those that keep the saltshakers full, to the Captain of the ship and to everyone else, every man and woman, whether human or giant, is of equal importance on this mission. We are all collectively the same. We have the common bond of being sentient brothers and sisters. This time we fly for everyone; all that live, all that have lived, and all that will live. May what we find be the long sought-after answer to the questions...*where* and *why*." He paused for effect. "Okay, enough of the speech, let's all interact and get to know our fellow travelers."

Some new crew members had never personally met a giant, so they sought out Mentar and his contingent of giants. The thirty members of the bridge crews, the principals and two backups, sought each other out and began talking. All five of the telemetry and navigation people wanted to learn how Melvin Faulkner, a veteran of Cosmos and the Omni-Star, worked out navigating back to the solar system from anywhere by using the main stars of the various constellations. Melvin's two backup personnel, and all three navigators on Cosmos, wanted to know. The procedure would be a valuable tool should the starship, for some reason, lose its bearing and become lost in space. Melvin, 71, beaming with accomplishment, wrote up the procedure, and downloaded the data to each of his colleagues.

Angie Baker, Copilot Cosmos, sought out Katy Baylor, computer systems expert on the bridge of the Omni-Star. "I saw the statuette at the museum here in the spaceport and your write-up. I looked for some of the Athenians myself when we were at Spaceport Zeta, but none were visiting while we were there. According to the ship's log, you had lunch with one of them."

"Yes. His name is Kaylan. Nice guy. Here, let me show you something." Katy pulled out her communicator and brought up the farewell note she received with the gift of the statuette. "This is the note he sent with the parting gift when we set sail for home. He had our security team deliver the gift to me after we had launched from the station."

Angie read the note:

Katy Baylor - Dream for me and I shall fly for you. Farewell, my friend from Earth.   Kaylan.

"Wow!" Angie said with feeling.

"Angie," Katy said. "The world has changed. There are so many expressions of life that its source has to be something magnificent. This will probably be my last mission. This is the big one, I just know it."

Colonel Austin, Colonel Stahls, and Mentar, took Akela to see the Moai that was transferred from the Moon to its present position as a marker at Mentar City. As they approached, Akela saw it from a distance, then stopped and stared momentarily. "Where did you get that!? It's identical to one of the markers, the pattern statues, of the transplants done by the science depart...."

Akela suddenly froze, glanced at Mentar, then walked up to the Moai, then around it, then looked at the back of it. There was no etching on it; no symbol identifying it. It seemed to be a copy of the original. "Mentar, it's you!" he said, looking up at the giant, "you're the transplant!"

"That's just the half of it," Jimmy interjected, "they," he pointed at Mentar, "transplanted us."

Akela's eyes went from Jimmy to Mentar, and then to the Moai. "The scientists on Concavia must have cut a second one to replace the original. But how did it get here?"

"By way of Zannia," Mentar said. "My ancient ancestors who escaped our dying planet had found it on Zannia and brought it with them. They had placed it at the entrance of the retirement city on Earth's moon. After our discovery in the chambers underneath the Moon, and we were established here on Earth, I had it brought here to Mentar City as a marker and a reminder of where we came from."

Akela's eyes went to Jimmy, then to Leslie, then up to Mentar. "If your kind was involved in transplanting or bringing these Earthlings into sentience, where did *you* get the catalyst?"

"Catalyst?"

"The deoxyribonucleic acid carrier solution."

"The DNA?" Jimmy muttered, looking at Mentar, "suspended in a carrier solution?" He looked back at Akela. "You must mean the amber liquid sealed in the bottles that were found in the lab on the Moon when we first discovered Mentar and his students asleep in the caves."

Akela nodded. "That's probably it but I don't know much about the science. During my trial I was also accused of plotting to steal some of that fluid. So, I knew it was important to their experiments."

Jimmy said. "We don't know where it originally came from but the Ship's Log on the ancient starship Zannia 2 listed it as part of the cargo taken from a disabled ship, with all crew long dead, found drifting between Zannia and our solar system."

Mentar added, "Apparently, after years of experimentation, our Zannian scientists figured out what it was and what it would do. We aren't sure, but their experiments must have contributed to the Earthlings coming to be."

Jimmy continued. "That's why we are going to Concavia. We are looking for answers. What has happened here in the solar system historically is a long story. We will fill you in on the way to your planet."

Chapter 10

LAUNCH

The Omni-Star and Cosmos rose from the Frank Gordon Space Flight Center into a clear blue sky amid no less than a million spectators surrounding the center for up to a mile out. The two half-mile-wide ships were easily followed with the naked eye up to virtually leaving the atmosphere. Some with powerful telescopes would eventually watch the two spacecrafts, flying in formation, arrive at the Kuiper Belt Vortex.

The starships paused for a few moments just above the atmosphere, hanging in space as if discussing a scenic route, while the computer specialists from each bridge set up the program and engaged the computers. The ships engaged power and began the journey with their sensors scanning far ahead for a clear path.

With the ships in route and everything in order, many of the crew made their way to the cargo hold for a close look at the Moai. A couple of the giants from Mentar City were seen pursing their lips trying to mimic the profile of the pattern statue. Beginning to draw a crowd, they ceased and employed a disarming smile with a sprinkle of self-consciousness.

Akela wasn't able to contribute much information regarding the specifics of the 'question' that was driving mission. He had seen the statues and carvings lined up across the front of the Hall of Records of the central government's science pavilion. In fact, that was what eventually inspired the political movement protesting it. That, and a couple of converts from the government ranks that contributed the information about the catalyst solution.

The movement began to take hold and grow, resulting eventually, in Akela's banishment. Akela was surprised to find that many of the citizenry of Concavia felt as he did. That fact aggravated the government's dealing with Akela, resulting in the ultimate sentence being handed down. Akela wondered if the movement continued. He would find out now. He needed to know. The price he had paid was high.

When the ship's chronometer indicated dawn of the second day, Mars was passing into the rear-view monitors of the armada. The scientists put the aft telescope of the Omni-Star on Cydonia to view the new dome. It was almost as noticeable as Olympus Mons. Mars was beginning to look promising; a place to live. The planet grew tiny very soon as the ships sailed on.

For the first time since the original mission to Zannia, a transfer from ship to ship was arranged for a lunch engagement and meeting. The players would be Mentar and his team to meet with the new riders from Mentar City, and Jimmy and his primary bridge crew, especially navigation, to confer with the team on

Cosmos. On the menu was Mentar's famous potato soup, ten large bowls and ten small ones. The meeting went well. The computer techs were satisfied with the formation-flying program and its performance.

The commanders, the seasoned, aging, Colonel Austin and the young, fresh Colonel Stahls, seemed as if they had been a space-faring team for a long time. After a meeting filled with expectation and motivation, the crew of the Omni-Star returned to their duties with their personal thoughts and hopes.

Aboard the Omni-Star—Main deck
Records Section

Dedra Allison didn't mind so much being called 'shorty,' when she was in high school and college. Her 4'11" frame was noticeable to everyone around and the 'handle' was always applied good-naturedly. Now, as a starship professional that 'handle' had all but faded away, especially since the crew had encountered the variety of species at Spaceport Zeta.

Dedra was a stickler for detail, a character trait that won her the position aboard the starship and with it, a chance to sail the heavens.

Now, here she was, continuing her job on this new far-reaching mission. Dedra entered the figures from her last survey of the bridge equipment readouts, along with the figures from engineering, into the computer system. She then transmitted a digital backup to the NASA permanent archives to be stored for posterity. As she recorded the completion of the transmission, there was a knock on the door of the office she shared with three other records specialists. The four of them staffed records around the clock on a floating 4-shift arrangement. She opened the door, then looked slightly downward. There stood Akela, all four-feet of him, smiling up at her. Dedra returned the smile, then her face showed question.

"Wonderful," Akela said and smiled again.

"Excuse me?"

"My English....I am still learning. Thank you...for helping me on Earth. You are wonderful."

Dedra smiled. "The English you speak is pretty good."

Akela smiled and simply waited, the tact of a diplomat. Dedra picked up on it, held up a finger, 'wait.' She stepped back, motioned for Akela to enter, then closed the door and stepped to the office supplies cabinet and took out an electronic device and turned it on. She positioned the device so Akela could see the translation on the screen. "While we were on Earth, we ordered an Italian-to-English and English-to-Italian translator to facilitate any records concerning you. You are speaking English well, but we wanted to make sure our records of conversations were accurate."

"Akela smiled broadly. "Will you have lunch with me?"

Dedra smiled and turned off the translator. "Yes."

George Manly and Steven Copeland, main deck security, watched the pair walk by. As they passed, they looked up at the two guards and smiled. Security returned the smile and nodded., then the older guard looked at his colleague. "I told you; he has a personality that attracts people."

"Yeah," Steven responded. "I'd like to know his pickup line."

"It's not a romantic thing; he has a family on Concavia. He's more like a politician. He shows appreciation to whoever can help him. You saw the way he handled himself in the conference hall when the colonel introduced him. If that guy fell off a cliff, he could talk his way out of hitting bottom."

Steven chuckled. "Yeah, but it remains to be seen if he can talk his way back onto his planet."

George watched the pair disappear into the lounge. "I'd say he has a good shot at it."

"He is a good talker," Steven commented, then smiled. "I like to be able to attract people like he does. I'm not a very good talker. I don't know all the cool stuff to say."

An older George Manly looked at his young friend and colleague. "Steven, the cool stuff to say to attract people is the plain truth. For instance, if you're trying to attract a girl, just go…"

"You mean Sheila Townsend."

George smiled, "The nurse in medical?"

"Yeah, she's pretty."

"Well then, just knock on her door and tell her you want to take her to dinner, but you don't know what to say."

"Just like that?"

"It's the truth, isn't it? You will be surprised just how far the plain truth will go."

At 7:00 p.m., Steven stopped twenty yards away from Sheila's quarters, took a couple of deep breaths, then approached her door and knocked. As he waited, his legs went electric. He wanted to run, but he didn't know if he could make it around the corner before she opened…too late.

"Oh, hi," Sheila said, looking up at the 6'4" security expert and smiling, "are you looking for a bad guy?"

Steven cleared his throat, then found his voice. "No, I'm here to pick you up and take you to dinner, but I don't know how to ask."

Sheila smiled again, then stepped back holding the door open. "Well, you're off to a good start. Come in. I need to brush my hair."

George Manly was off duty and taking his break sitting at a table in the aft lounge having dinner. He looked up and watched his young partner and Sheila Townsend enter the lounge and locate a table. When they were seated, Steven began talking. Sheila was smiling and nodding, speaking a word or two now and then.

"For a fellow that don't know what to say, he's doing an awful lot of talking," George mused and smiled to himself. *"George, the matchmaker,"* he thought.

Chapter 11

THE VORTEX

The Omni-Star and Cosmos were counting off the last hours of the deceleration phase of the Earth-to-Vortex Telemetry Program. In just 78 hours it would show zero. The vortex was just over three days away. The bridge crew was checking sensor readings and frequent visuals through the massive windshields of the two starships. So far, the sensors were clear and there was nothing through the giant window but a star-studded black velvet tapestry with a depth reaching infinity.

When the duo of ships came to rest, the vortex would be 100 miles dead ahead. It would appear to be a swirling bank of white fluffy clouds shaped like a lamp shade. It measured miles across; the manifestation of the presence of dark matter and dark energy which doubled in density at every wormhole vortex. Of course, wormholes were junctions of two of the main energy rivers remaining in place and flowing through the galaxy, for some still unknown reasons. It was a mystery even more tantalizing than the age-old question; *why does electricity flow*? It's very beneficial and reliable, even though unknown.

Colonel Austin keyed the ship-to-ship communications link. "Colonel Stahls, after we have the ships stabilized, bring your bridge crew, your engine room staff, and safety people over and let's have a prep meeting before we enter the wormhole."

"Yes, sir. We'll be on our way as soon as we're stabilized."

An hour later, all parties were sitting in the conference room of the Omni-Star. Jimmy began. "We are about to fly forty lightyears in a wormhole. If we flew at light speed through open space, that would be almost 90 years round trip away from home. But we can be thankful it's only about forty days in the marvelous wormhole system, with two stops in route.

As we discussed, we will enter separately, staying far enough apart to remain safe. The Omni-Star will go first. Before you follow, you will give us the planned half-hour head start. That will provide the necessary separation between the ships.

When we exit at each vortex, we will engage power and move the ship away from the vortex for obvious reasons. We will spend a couple of days at the Station Keeping power setting for a review, more if we need it. Any questions or comments?"

"Yes," Colonel Stahls said. "According to the androids in the instructional seminar, the ships will be propelled at equal velocity, so a half-hour separation will be plenty, and it won't be so long to wait to know the status of the sister ship. Our crews can share ships' status when we regroup at each vortex."

"Anything else?"

"Yes, sir," Henry Alderman, Cosmos safety officer said. "They told us in wormhole training that quantum communications had been sketchy through the wall of the tunnel to the outside. They also said they had not tried communicating between ships when both were inside the wormhole, since other species don't fly their ships as close to each other as we will be doing. I think we should check communications, ship-to-ship, right after we enter the wormhole. It's best to know early-on if we can talk."

"Good point," Jimmy said. "We'll do that. Maybe we set a trend for others. Once you're inside, try a communications check with us. If it doesn't work, we could have radio silence in between each vortex. That's a long time to be isolated. We'll also have our communications team experiment with frequencies that may give us reliable communications through the wall of the wormhole. If not...we'll wing it!"

The crew laughed.

"As we discussed about the two stops on the way," Bruce offered. "The first one is eight lightyears, then eighteen, then fourteen to the end. If we can't talk inside the wormhole, and quantum systems are unreliable, the longest isolation will be eighteen days. Colonel, I think that the river of dark energy may well disrupt radio signals, even quantum signals. A field of energy that will propel a ship at wormhole speeds has to have some serious density and cohesion. We had better be prepared for radio silence."

"You're probably right, Bruce. But we'll check it."

There was silence for a moment or two. "Okay," Colonel Austin said, "anybody else?"

"Colonel," Dave Walters said, "As Pilot of Cosmos, I know how crucial it is to make sure I enter the same tunnel as the Omni-Star. Otherwise, we'll end up somewhere else in the galaxy. We've discussed the multiple tunnels leading from this vortex and the schematic shows the one we need is the first tunnel on the right as we enter the vortex. If it's alright, I'd like to crowd your ship very closely at the vortex so I can visually watch the turn you make. The Auto Pilot should handle it fine but, you never know…sometimes mistakes happen. But…that is one mistake we can't afford to make."

"Point well taken, Dave. Before leaving Earth, we did make sure the Wormhole System Diagram was downloaded into each ship's computer data base. Both of you safety officers need to make sure our entries into the wormhole happens as outlined by Mr. Walters. Okay," Jimmy concluded, "if there's nothing else, let's make final preparations to enter the wormhole tomorrow morning and begin our journey."

The Omni-Star
Entering the Vortex

"Cosmos," Sheldon Darcy said, "please note the transmitted image. The four tunnels at this vortex are on plane with our solar system. We are entering the rightmost tunnel. It's right next to the wall of the vortex."

"Acknowledged," Dave Walters said as the Omni-Star faded into the mist. "We have it on visual and will be following you in, in thirty minutes."

All Sheldon heard was *Acknowledged*...then the radios went silent. They felt the dark matter wrap around the Omni-Star and accelerate it forward at an incredible speed. The pilot then throttled back to ZERO THRUST and postured the ship for eight days of wormhole travel. Jacob Watkins, Communications, watched the clock. At thirty-five minutes, he keyed the intercom to the bridge. "Colonel, thirty-five minutes. Cosmos has launched into the tunnel. Channel open, sir."

"Acknowledged," Colonel Austin said, then keyed Quantum Communications. "Cosmos, this is the Omni-Star, come in please."

There was only a sporadic faint raspy sound coming from the speakers. Jacob turned the gain control to full volume. Colonel Austin keyed again. "Cosmos, this is the Omni-Star, come in please."

Still only silence with more pronounced static sounds.

Jimmy released the button. "Okay, Bruce is right. Dark energy disrupts the communication signals. We will always have to be postured to function with no ship-to-ship contact while traveling the wormhole."

Aboard Cosmos
Entering the Wormhole

Communications keyed the intercom to the bridge. "Colonel Stahls, thrust is at zero. The Quantum Communications channel to the Omni-Star is open."

Leslie keyed the communications equipment to the sister starship. "Omni-Star, this is Cosmos, come in please." A raspy static came from the speakers. Leslie keyed again. "Repeat, Omni-Star, this is Cosmos, respond please."

Nothing.

"Just as we suspected," Leslie said. "It's the dark energy. Apparently, it overwhelms the radio energy."

The colonel was quiet for a few moments. "We can't communicate through the wormhole. I wonder if we can call outside of the wormhole. That would be a relatively small amount of dark energy between the ship and the clear space surrounding the tunnel. And, if I remember correctly from Interstellar Training, the lower frequency band will penetrate material better than the higher frequencies...like the ship-to-ship band. Communications, switch to the Low Frequency Band Range and set me up to call NASA on Earth."

The two communications techs looked at each other, shrugged their shoulders and dialed in the settings. "Channel open, sir."

Colonel Stahls keyed the mike again. "NASA headquarters, this is Cosmos, come in please."

A few seconds later. *"Go ahead, Cosmos."*

A cacophony of hoots and *yeas* went up on Cosmos.

"Colonel, you're a genius!" Dave Walters exclaimed.

"You can thank my grandfather," Leslie responded, "He was a Signal Corps officer in World War 2. He told me stories of how they communicated with their primitive equipment. His team was once hiding in a cave from the Germans and needed to call for air support. He knew that lower frequencies would penetrate denser material, like the cave wall. So, he bottomed out the dial on his radio and kept calling until someone happened to tune past that low frequency. They relayed his call and a flight of British Spitfires soon arrived to clear a path for their escape.

"I'm a student of Cosmos, this modern starship, but I'm smart enough to listen to the old 'tried-and-true' methods used by the Greatest Generation." Leslie keyed the mic once more. "NASA, this is Colonel Stahls, we are in the wormhole and we are unable to radio ship-to-ship while submerged in this river of dark energy. Please radio the Omni-Star on the low band and inform them that we are on schedule and following thirty minutes behind them. Let them know everything is fine. Then take any messages they may have for us."

"Understood, Cosmos, standby."

Aboard the Omni-Star

In the effort to contact Cosmos, the communications techs had left the volume setting at maximum on the Quantum Communication equipment. Suddenly, a booming transmission energized the low band receiver. *"Omni-Star, this is NASA: we have a message from Cosmos: please advise when you are ready to copy."*

The two techs bumped into each other trying to get to the controls to adjust the gain. Jimmy heard the reverberating transmission. He keyed the link. "Go ahead, NASA."

"Colonel, we received a message from Cosmos. They are unable to reach you due to interference from the dark energy in the wormhole. However, they are able to transmit out of the tunnel on this Low Frequency band. They have asked us to act as a connecting link for ship-to-ship communications. Their message reads: We are on schedule, thirty minutes behind you. Everything is fine. End of message. Have you a response, Omni-Star?"

"Yes," Jimmy said. "Send this: Great job on establishing communications. We're glad to hear the good report on your ship's status. We are in order here as well. We will contact you, via the NASA link, every six hours while traveling the tunnel. Omni-Star signing off."

"Roger, Colonel, will inform Cosmos."

As the minutes turned into an hour, then two, life aboard the starship gradually went back to normal.

The general sentiment aboard the Omni-Star was complete trust of the wormhole system. The Zylons and others that frequented the spaceport had used it for eons. It was a common highway for travelers from many planets. Now, Earth was part of the family.

Akela approached the bridge and seated himself in one of the extra seats provided, facing the windshield. Colonel Austin noticed his demeanor, as he seemed unusually quiet. Jimmy got up from the command chair and moved over and sat down beside Akela. "Well, we're on our way," he said, then turned and looked through the windshield also.

Akela, now fairly proficient in English after months of interaction, glanced at the commander, then back to the cloudy-appearing walls of the giant tube racing by the starship. "Colonel, I remember twenty-six years ago, being in this tunnel, going the other way. The government arranged my passage on a freighter. The freighter received some type of compensation for obliging me with a seat on their ship. They weren't interested in any details, they just did their duty and delivered me to Spaceport Zeta. Although the wormhole travel lasted only a few weeks, the journey to Zeta seemed to have lasted forever. After the crew dropped me off, they stayed overnight, then moved on to wherever their business took them."

"You told us about the group that was protesting on Concavia. Why did they prosecute just you?"

Akela glanced at the colonel, "I come from a long line of protesters."

"I don't understand."

"Well, 200 years ago, my great-grandfather was a quetagarian. He…

"Wait…a quetagarian…what's that?"

"In Earth terms, I think you would call him a, uh, farmer. Yes, I believe that's the term you would use. Anyway, he was one of the first to protest government interference in the farming industry. The government wanted to transition to genetically modified, machine produced food. He and many other farmers rallied the other communities together and stood their ground. The government backed off but recorded him as a trouble-maker.

"I guess the only good thing I could say about the government is that they allowed my family to say goodbye at the departure depot on Concavia when I was forced to leave the planet. My son, Galen, was adolescent; he's 40 now; a man. He was fourteen then, and when I hugged him for the last time, I told him I was coming back. I said I was going to figure out a way to come back home."

"Well," Jimmy said, smiling, "you found a way. You kept that promise. All you have to do now is get past the red tape."

"Red tape?"

"Yes, Red Tape is a term we use to indicate the complicated administrative rules governments create to control about every function we are involved in. Your *red tape* will be figuring out how to get your government to set aside your conviction or how to get forgiveness and be cleared to return home. And, if things go badly for you in your attempt, we would be happy to take your family aboard and back to Earth with you."

"I am grateful for that." Akela said, then paused a moment. "However, I hope to be able to resolve this and return to my family there on Concavia. It's home."

"I understand. I just wanted you to know that the option is open to you."

"I think I can get back home." Akela smiled. "I've been working on the speech for 26 years."

"Good luck."

"Thank you. If I fail, I will take you up on that invitation. I like Earth. On Earth, if you get tired of the people around you, you can just move to the next country. The people will speak a different language and, in some cases, even be a different color, although I didn't see any grey people on Earth." Akela said as if making a normal observation.

"Yeah. That's Earth."

DAN HOLT & MAX HOLT

Chapter 12

SPACEPORT ARRIVAL

Eight days later
Junction Vortex #1

The bridge crew and a hundred or so of the ship's crew, strapped in on the main deck, and the remaining travelers eyeing monitors throughout the ship, watched the giant ring of mist, the end of the tunnel, pass by the ship. The sudden stop was as exciting as the crew had experienced in earlier exits from wormholes. The ship quickly came to the Station Keeping power setting, floating just outside the vortex. There was little sensation of inertial force that the normal human senses used to tell a person what was coming. The visual and the reality did not match. A wave of disorientation swept through the crew. However, it quickly dissipated as the sight of the star-studded heavens was, as always, there, and the same.

"Mr. Walters," Jimmy said, "engage power and move us a mile away from the tunnel opening."

"Yes, sir, moving the ship now."

Shortly, the ship was a mile to the side of the transit tunnel, facing it, waiting for Cosmos to appear.

Sharon Millar, safety officer, looked at the ship's chronometer. "Ten minutes."

Akela glanced at the Colonel and spoke in relatively good English. "Colonel, you've seen this before, but it is still amazing to me. It will look like the ship just suddenly materializes out of nothing. One second it's empty space, the next, there's a ship."

Jimmy nodded. "Yes, I've seen it but I am still amazed each time."

Everyone's eyes locked on the tunnel opening and waited. Suddenly, eleven minutes and a few seconds later, Cosmos was hanging completely motionless in space centered in Omni-Star's windshield.

Jimmy keyed the radio. "Cosmos...You are just over a minute late. Everything okay?"

"Yes. I think we used up the extra minute maneuvering into the tunnel at the start."

"Understood."

Radar and sensor monitoring keyed into the bridge. "Colonel, there's a structure behind us. It's stationary, about twelve miles in diameter, five miles away."

"It's a space station," Akela said, "a small one. Ships can't enter, but they have moorings outside for shuttles and variable width airlocks to accommodate different vessels. We stopped here twenty-six years ago and had a bowl of Mentar soup. That recipe has really spread throughout this part of the galaxy. I had the small bowl."

Laughter rippled through the two ships. Mentar was listening on the Intercom and glanced around at his colleagues and smiled.

"It's really good," Akela added.

"Yeah," Jimmy said. "That recipe came from Mentar."

Akala was surprised. "You mean our Mentar...uh...I mean Commander Mentar, on board now?!

"Yes."

"Really?!"

"Yes. In fact, Mentar, of Mentar Soup fame, is the one aboard now and he even tweaked our recipe with a slight improvement, some kind of new spices."

Akala still couldn't believe it. "You mean that our Mentar is the same Mentar of Mentar Soup; small, medium, and large?"

Jimmy laughed. "One in the same."

Akela smiled. "I had no idea that our Mentar was the creator of the famous Mentar soup? Amazing!"

A deep voice came from the intercom: "Actually, I didn't create the recipe. The *little ones* of Earth did when they rescued us giants on the Moon long ago. The variation of Mentar Soup, small, medium, and large, came from the kitchens of an interplanetary ship called Discovery, many years ago."

"So, it's called Mentar soup because you were the first one to eat it?"

"No, the first one to eat it was one of my students, Kronos. The first time he ate it, they didn't know his name, so they just called him BIG JOHN."

Akela laid his hands flat on his bald head, then laid his forehead down on the padded console in front of him. "I'm confused. Why is it called Mentar soup?"

"It's a long story," Jimmy said, smiling. "It has to do with a series of events. We'll tell you the whole thing on our next leg through the tunnel system. Right now, let's go inside and enjoy some of it while we check out this spaceport. In the interest of time, only a small group of us will go. The rest of the armada's occupants can order it in the on-board cafeteria. We will be visiting all the facilities we encounter in this wormhole system; briefly, at least."

Colonel Austin keyed the ship-to-ship intercom. "Colonel Stahls...follow us in your Command Shuttle. Let's do a brief visit of this space station. The leaders here will be meeting their first Zannians and Earthlings."

"Yes, sir. Soon, Earth is going to have to build a space station at the Kuiper Belt Vortex. I don't think we will ever become a successful galaxy trading partner without it."

"You're right. Perhaps we will have to start with a small one. This one here is much smaller than Zeta."

As the starships approached, it came into view that there were mechanical moorings with tunnels and airlocks to accommodate smaller ships and shuttles. Three other starships were parked on the other side of the spaceport. The shuttles attached to the moorings were obviously from those ships. The Omni-Star and Cosmos shuttles approached the moorings on their side of the space station.

With the ships at Station Keeping, Colonel Austin keyed the ship-to-ship again. "Colonel Stahls, set your intercom to OPEN, and monitor.

"Acknowledged," came from the speakers.

Jimmy radioed the spaceport with their designation listed on the Wormhole Map in the ship's data base. It was the second vortex on the Orion Spur, servicing the sector around the star, Procyon. They had been in existence for hundreds of years, so he assumed they would have the same automatic translators built into their external communications systems as Zeta. "Spaceport Procyon 2, we are the commanders of the Omni-Star and Cosmos, asking permission to dock and enter."

"Roger, Earth ships," a mechanical voice speaking perfect English responded, *"you are welcome."*

"Thank you," Jimmy responded, "how did you know we were from Earth?"

"Other than your ships' markings, it was your magnetic signature. Your ships have a very strong magnetic reading. The magnetometers quickly identified you. Welcome to Procyon 2. Enter by shuttle when ready. How many shuttles will be mooring?"

Jimmy thought for a moment. "Four."

Roger. Attach to Moorings 90 through 94. The airlock attachments will automatically adjust to your fittings."

"Thank you, Procyon 2. Be advised, we have ten of the giants of Zannia in our landing party."

"Understood. We know of them and welcome them."

Colonel Austin disconnected and turned to Bruce. "That name, Procyon 2, I've heard it before. I believe the android, Seven, mentioned it while we were engaged in idle conversation. I didn't pay much attention at the time. What planet or planets support this facility?"

Jimmy turned to Akela. "Akela, do you know what planet or planets built this spaceport?"

"Yes, Commander. It was built by and is maintained by Procyon 1, a planet about a half lightyear away. They specialize in androids. Seven was designed, built, and programmed there. Procyon 1 supplies the Zylons with androids, and anyone else who makes the necessary financial arrangements."

"I'll bet they're expensive," Bruce said.

"No doubt," Jimmy agreed. "Let's go check out their spaceport."

Jimmy turned back to the intercom and keyed Mentar's quarters. "Mentar, you and your team board your shuttle and let's check out the spaceport. Bring Zoll. I want to show off his Zolaadine body."

"Colonel," Mentar responded, "are you planning to do some business here?"

"Perhaps later. I think it's a good idea to let them know we have things of value. Zolaadine and Neodymium.

"Understood."

"Leslie," Jimmy said through the intercom.

"Yes, Colonel."

"Have the giants from Mentar City board their shuttle and accompany us into the spaceport. You pick five of your crew to accompany you and fly your shuttle in with us."

"Will do, Colonel. We'll meet you inside."

DAN HOLT & MAX HOLT

Chapter 13

PROCYON 2

Shore leave

Katy Baylor requested and received permission to pilot Jimmy's shuttle from the Omni-Star to Procyon 2. She, though a certified pilot, didn't get many opportunities to log flight hours at the helm of an excursion craft. Her expertise always kept her on the larger ship's bridge. Her main duty, operating the power and control computers of the Omni-Star, was a full-time job.

Katy settled into the pilot's seat of the shuttle. She held her hands in the prayer position, blew on them, rubbed them together, then gently placed them on the controls. "Small corrections and gentle pressure on the throttle," she whispered, quoting her instructor of many years ago. The Colonel's personal shuttle was a delight to steer. It had very low mass and a full-size rotor pod for power, making its movements prompt, clean, and precise.

On board was the colonel along with First Officer Bruce Wilson, Akela, Copilot Timothy Dalton, and main deck security, George Manly. Katy wondered how the colonel chose who was going on the shuttle to Procyon 2. His selections always seem to make sense.

As per the colonel's instructions, she approached the moorings they were assigned. She changed the power setting to Station Keeping and then nudged the shuttle toward the mooring, gently 'kissing' the airlock coupling. An audible *click* indicated a firm docking. The other shuttles followed her example.

The colonel gave Katy a smile and a nod, indicating a job well done. Katy let out her breath, then, placed the power controls back at Station Keeping.

After confirming that all four shuttles had docked, Jimmy keyed the mic. "All shuttle personnel switch to personal communicators for staying in contact. Their Reception Area should be obvious…let's all meet there."

He got a "Roger," form the other shuttles.

They all entered the spaceport at about the same time. The tunnel exits were near some sort of android staging area. The androids looked up when the new arrivals passed by, as if they were curious, an unusual trait for machines.

"Very sophisticated programming," Jimmy thought. When the giants entered, one of the androids spoke into a communicator, probably letting everyone in the spaceport know that there was something special to see today, the largest known humanoids.

The nearest android turned to Colonel Austin and spoke in English. *"Internal transports are available if you require."*

"Excellent," Jimmy said. "I'm Colonel Austin commanding the Omni-Star," Jimmy turned to Leslie, "this is Colonel Stahls commanding Cosmos, and you are…?"

"I am Linguist."

"Well, Linguist, does your name indicate you to be the translator here?"

"Yes, I am programmed with every known language in this part of the galaxy."

"Great! The station is very accommodating. Please take us to a lounge to enjoy a bowl of your Mentar soup.

Linguist paused only a split second. *"Yes Commander. I'll call for the transports."*

Minutes later, three transports arrived at the edge of the landing deck. One had regular seating to accommodate twelve passengers and two had seats appropriate for the giants that seated six each. "How about that," Jimmy said. "Transports built for the giants."

"Yes," Linguist said. *They were designed and constructed when Procyon 1 learned of Zannia. The Station Commander felt sure your species and theirs would be transiting this way eventually. They have been parked ever since, that is, until today."*

The parties boarded the transports for the trip to the lounge for a meal. The android took a moment and noted that Zoll was sitting on the front row of seats on the transport, beside Mentar, with his feet dangling above the floor. His height was noted; more than twice that of a citizen of Earth; about half that of a Zannian.

As Linguist began the trip to the lounge, his mind transmitted the specifications to the Procyon 2 lab, and the main design computer began working on an adjustable seat for transport use.

Soon, they arrived at a lounge about a mile into the spaceport. The décor and atmosphere were largely identical to Zeta.

"Colonel," Bruce said, "notice that they have tables for the Zannians."

Jimmy looked at the four tables so constructed to accommodate the 40-foot tall Mentar and company. "They must have gotten the specs from Zeta and went ahead and prepared for the inevitable. Those tables work for Zannians and the average humanoid, six feet tall. There were varying size tables as well. Zolaadine Man was able to seat himself. He attracted some attention. Many were curious at the early design of the robot, especially his hardened body and general shape.   But his movements and speech were equivalent to the modern androids, a noticeable trait.

While they were waiting for their orders to be served, a transport pulled up to the lounge entrance and an officer of the Stationmaster Corps got out and looked around the group. "Colonel Austin?"

Several hands pointed at Jimmy. The officer quickly found the commander's graying temples and electric eyes. Jimmy extended his hand, and it was taken by the five-foot tall Procyonian. He shook Colonel Austin's hand energetically and smiled. "Welcome to Spaceport Procyon 2. I'm Atmos. We've been serving Mentar soup, small, medium, and large for over thirty years. It's very popular."

The words that the colonel was hearing were delayed a second or so behind the station representative's mouth movements. At first, it was disorienting to focus on what was being said. Then he noticed that the android's mouth was moving in sync with the words he was hearing. Jimmy frowned, looking one to the other, the stationmaster officer to the android, then back to the officer. He had heard only one voice.

The stationmaster's representative picked up on the commander's confusion. "Colonel, the pitch of my voice is above human hearing. That's why you are experiencing the delay. The android is repeating what I am saying to you, changing it to your voice frequency."

"That's amazing. Is there anybody else, ah, any other planets that can talk to you directly?"

"We've encountered one, so far, that can talk with us directly. The Athenians, the flyers, can hear our voices. Many centuries ago, when our planet built this spaceport, voice frequency was the first thing they had to deal with. It's what prompted the developing of the androids. It was the voice pitch problem that led to specializing in sophisticated androids to be marketed and, of course, to be installed here as part of our spaceport equipment, or put more appropriately, our spaceport staff."

"I'm impressed," Jimmy responded, "It's a very effective solution."

Four androids began ferrying bowls of soup from the kitchen to the tables seating seventeen souls from planet Earth and five from Zannia, along with a unique robot, Zoll. Jimmy looked around at the group preparing to indulge. "Atmos," he inquired, "I'm curious. Why is Mentar soup listed as small, medium, and large?"

"It's not the obvious designation one would think. The quantity is 'all you can eat' on any order. The *ingredients* are sized, small, medium, and large, according to the patron that will be enjoying it."

Jimmy glanced at Akela's and Mentar's mouths and smiled to himself.

The group began enjoying the popular cuisine. It was a group that had just learned that voice frequency is not necessarily a given.

Chapter 14

FRIENDS IN NEED

The crews mounted the transports, looking for an informative tour of the spaceport. The android pilot turned to the new visitors. *"With your permission, we'll show you our specialty. We always show our new visitors our android lab and museum displays."*

"Yes," Jimmy said, "we would like to see that."

With that, the caravan began moving. About a mile down an arrow-straight aisle, on the left, was a sitting area. As a backdrop, there was a large semicircle of spacesuits hanging on a latticework rack. There were several different configurations; some bulky, perhaps designed for extreme temperature or extreme pressure situations; some trim and close-fitting. Two on the display were strikingly similar to the first suits used by the crew that went on the original Moon Mission and discovered Mentar and his students.

Linguist brought the transports to a stop. "This is one of our collections. Some of these suits date back prior to the building of Procyon 2." Moments later, Linguist resumed the tour. Shortly, he made a right turn, then increased speed. Several sitting areas and floor-to-floor escalators went by, then the crew saw a club-type facility coming up on the right. "Is that a Spirits and Song Club?" Jimmy inquired.

"Yes, that's what they call it at Zeta." Linguist responded. "Here it's called the High Frequency Inn."

"Clever name," Jimmy said, smiling.

The android slowed the transport and came to a stop in front of the building. *"This is also an entertainment facility, the same as the Spirit's and Song on Zeta. Would you like to go in?"*

"Yes," Jimmy said, "let's check it out. We've got to order at least one drink."

The troupe from Earth and Zannia entered the club and were seated by the android attendees. There was a darkened atmosphere and soft music coming from a console on one side of the facility. There were, perhaps, thirty humanoids sitting in groups; that is, all but three individuals that were occupying tables alone, sipping drinks and sitting quietly. Colonel Austin addressed Linguist. "Linguist, you order the first round; the specialty of the house."

"Specialty of the house, Commander?"

"Yes, what's the signature drink, the most popular?"

"Ah, the drinks most served."

"Yes."

Linguist placed the order. Momentarily, two androids began placing the drinks in front of the guests. Jimmy looked from drink to drink at the tiny columns of smoke. "Definitely Spirits and Song."

Linguist smiled, then looked at Jimmy. *"Take a sip of it."*

Jimmy did so then, looked at Linguist, and raised his eyebrows. The android smiled again. *"We get that reaction from almost everybody. This drink, called the High Frequency Special, is forty percent spirits."*

"You gotta have a gimmick," Jimmy mused, then looked at Linguist. "It's good, it has a good taste," he added and then glanced at the giants from Mentar City blowing smoke across the table then holding up the drinks and looking at them.

Katy took a couple of sips of her drink. Then, looking around the club, her eyes found one of the individuals sitting alone. She watched the patron momentarily. He would take a sip of his drink, set it down, then idly wring his hands together as if wrestling with a problem. Something stirred inside her. She got up from her table and approach him, a humanoid, a little over seven feet tall, with a full beard, full head of hair, and a ponytail reaching down to his waist behind him.

When she stepped up to his table, he was about to take another sip of his drink and repeat his ritual. He set his drink back down and looked at Katy. His physical height had them almost eye level with each other. Katy smiled, looked around the club, located Linguist, then gestured for him to come to her aide. Momentarily, he was standing at her side. Katy looked up at the android. "Linguist, I want to talk to his man, I need for you to translate for me."

"He speaks your language," Linguist responded.

"He speaks English!?"

"Yes, he's a representative for the Planetary Alliance based on Zeta. He studies the new planets that join the Federation. He speaks about a dozen languages; English is one of them."

"Great! Thank you, Linguist," Katy said, turning and smiling at the man seated at the table. He returned her smile. She found him attractive and manly of stature. She turned back to Linguist. "Shew...go away," she whispered, gesturing with her hands.

Linguist activated a dozen servos, looking for a facial expression to fit the moment, finding none, he simply returned to the party going on across the room.

George Manly, main deck security, having a keenly developed observer's eye, smiled at the android's first mystery lesson about women.

Katy gestured toward the chair at the lone man's table. "May I?"

He indicated the chair, palm up, and nodded. Katy seated herself.

"What can I do for you, young lady," he said in a resonant baritone voice.

"Oh, I like you already," Katy said. "My name is Katy Baylor. I'm from Earth."

"I'm Professor Emmitt Bonyaar of the Institute of Space Research on Cyrus A."

"Cyrus A?"

"Actually, a planet orbiting Cygnus A."

"You are a college professor?"

"Yes. I lecture in this quadrant on the dynamics of space expansion and development."

Katy smiled, "I'm a computer technician on a star ship, the Omni-Star."

The professor nodded and smiled. Katy looked down at the table, paused a few moments, then made a decision. She looked up at the handsome teacher. "Professor, what was bothering you earlier?"

"What do you mean?"

"I know I shouldn't pry into your personal business, but I noticed you wringing your hands like something's bothering you. I hope it's not too serious."

Professor Bonyaar held Katy's eyes for a long moment. "Thank you for the sentiment. I didn't know I was that obvious. I haven't heard from my daughter in over a year."

"Oh, I'm sorry. What happened?"

"She's probably fine. She left with a group of researchers; a group of youngsters from the Institute, to explore the star system of the flyers, the Athenians. We were so close while she was growing up and now it seems that she just went silent."

"Some of our young do the same thing when they are growing into adulthood. They are finally on their own and experiencing life and don't realize how time is passing. Not to be insulting or anything but, have you tried calling her through Zeta?"

"No. Not yet. She never did like me checking up on her."

"Professor Bonyaar, I met the Athenians at Zeta, in the museum, six of them."

"Really!?'

"Yes. Our group from Earth was touring the museum at the time. When I found out from Seven that they were there, I asked to meet them.

"I'm not surprised," the Professor interjected and smiled.

Katy returned the smile. "Seven called and arranged it. The Athenians were in the library at the time doing some research themselves. Six of them flew to the museum to meet our party from Earth. Their leader's name was Kaylan. They are a nice species, I like them."

"I'm glad to hear that."

"Why don't you call Athena and get in contact with your daughter? Tell her you met somebody that visited with the Athenians at Zeta and you were wondering how her research is going? Ask her if she's met Kaylan yet. He's one of the dignitaries on Athena. That's not checking up on her, it's checking up on the group's research."

The professor straightened and smiled. "Katy Baylor, Earth has got to be an interesting place. I'm going to my quarters and make a quantum call."

Chapter 15

BIRTHPLACE

The touring group said goodbye to the High Frequency Inn and headed for the Android Lab and Museum. When the group passed through the entrance to the museum and lab complex, it became obvious that the facility was a promotional venue for the androids marketed by the spaceport. There were androids dating from the beginning of the highly developed android society to the present sophistication of the machines. However, where the actual design and programming took place was behind closed doors. Most of the development and production facilities had been move here from Procyon 1 in recent years.

The engineering and marketing groups showed a particular interest in Zoll and quizzed the Zannians at length. They would be calling to make arrangements for meetings concerning the Zolaadine available on their home planet.

Jimmy knew that when Earth reached the point of planning a spaceport at the Kuiper Belt Vortex, Procyon 1, the supplier of the popular androids, would be part of the endeavor. What a fascinating future.

As an unfolding future of Earth played in the colonel's mind, the image of Concavia, from Spaceport Zeta's library records, took forefront.

"Linguist," he said, "take us to our shuttles. Your spaceport is magnificent and I'm glad to have seen it, but I have a mission I must complete."

"Yes, Colonel," the android said and began the journey through the spaceport back to the landing area.

Upon arrival, the colonel gathered his fellow space farers together. "My fellow adventurers, let us return to our ships and the mission at hand."

Chapter 16

SAILING ON

The Omni-Star and Cosmos hovered side-by-side at the Procyon 2 Vortex. "Okay," Jimmy said, "notify us via NASA when you enter the wormhole. This time we have eighteen lightyears to travel before we can regroup. We are already twice as far from home as we have ever been. This one is the greatest distance we'll be traveling separated from each other. The next time we see each other, we will be twenty-six lightyears from Earth. Let's exercise due caution. The Omni-Star is entering the wormhole now."

The ship was, once again, tugged forward at a staggering velocity, with the engines reduced to Station Keeping power. At the thirty-five-minute mark, the NASA transmission came regarding Cosmos. She was on time and sailing as planned. Life aboard the starships slowly became normal, again. The eighteen-day stint was on and all aboard settled down to their respective routines.

With the ship underway, Akela came out of his quarters and made his way across the main deck and approached the bridge. "Colonel," he said to Jimmy, "tell me about Mentar soup. How did it actually come to be?"

Jimmy smiled, got up from the command chair and accompanied Akela to the seating area beside the bridge. Seated, he began:

"Half a century ago, on Earth's moon, the galley of Discovery, an interplanetary ship, created Mentar soup to feed Mentar and his fellow giants as they were awakened from suspended animation. The first one awakened was a student of Mentar's, named Kronos, a teenager. When the Earth-people discovered that Kronos was a youngster, they sought and found a mature giant, which happened to be Mentar, and awakened him to get some information on who the giants actually were and why they were entombed in animation units in caves underneath Earth's moon.

"That's when the soup was created. Since the Earth crews had no idea what the giants' food preferences were, they figured that potato soup was nourishing but benign enough as not to harm them. As it turned out, the giants had eaten similar vegetables before and really liked it. Then later, much later, Earth built a large starship, so the giants could return to their home planet. They named it **Little One**, in honor of the smaller Earthlings that built it. They still refer to us as *little ones*."

Akela smiled. "I guess they would have called me *tiny one*."

Jimmy chuckled, "Maybe." He continued his story. "A few years later, Earth also built Cosmos, the ship following us in the wormhole right now. As time passed, Mentar returned to Earth in Starship Little One to get his son, who had been found asleep with another group of giants submerged in the ocean beside Easter Island. I'm sure you remember that story during your orientation on Earth."

Akela nodded. "Yes, that was an amazing story of survival. And those hundreds of Moai they carved as a marker were unbelievable!"

Jimmy continued. "During Mentar's stay, our government decided to establish a Human Colony on Zannia, just as the giants had done on Earth. After the colonists were selected and a journey to Mentar's home planet was arranged for Little One and our newest starship at the time...Cosmos.

"Before setting out on that journey home, Mentar contacted Discovery and requested a copy of that soup recipe. During the journey to Zannia, a mishap occurred and both ships lost power due to a freak accident causing the engines to shut down. The shuttle bay was open on Little One. A free-floating toolbox bumped a control panel and released Mentar's personal shuttle out of the ship. By the time the emergency had been rectified, his shuttle had floated out the hangar door and was lost in deep space.

"Years later, while visiting Spaceport Zeta, we found Mentar's shuttle. The Altairians had found it and brought it to the spaceport and put it in the museum. While we were visiting there and touring the museum, we discovered it, and reclaimed it for Mentar. Thus, the recipe for Mentar soup, having been lost in space, became famous."

Akela looked out the windshield of the Omni-Star for a long moment.

"I can see why…it's really good!"

Cydonia, on Mars
Dark of Night

Elliot Scanlon and Will Proctor looked through the temporary transparent canopy they had installed over the excursion rover. Looking out they could see Cydonia in the distance, almost at the horizon. They had boarded the rover vehicle to drive out into the blackness of night to take another look at the star that was shining on Concavia. Since the two-ship mission launched, everyone on Earth and Mars was keeping watch. From where they were parked on the red planet's surface, they could see the topmost beacon on Discovery, blinking every five seconds. She was parked by the dome to supply the needs of the builders on Mars. Terraforming the planet was well under way.

Elliot turned off the power circuits of the rover and allowed the dark to take over completely. They looked up through the canopy and began scanning the blazing stars, looking farther into the Orion Spiral Arm of the galaxy. "There it is," Will said, pointing. "Trappist 1, the orange one."

They focused on the tiny point of light for a few moments. Elliot imagined that he could see two tiny pin-dots, one chasing the other, closing on it. He couldn't of course, but, with some imagination, his eyes could arrange it.

"They're way out there now," Will said, "a long way from home."

"Yeah," Elliot agreed, "and they're only about halfway."

Will shifted his position. "Has anybody thought about what to do if they don't come back?"

"Don't come back!?"

"Yeah. If something bad happens and things go wrong."

Elliot frowned, "They sent two ships. It's not likely that something bad would happen to both of them. They could all get in one and come home."

"I know," Will added. "I'm just saying. Suppose we lost contact and they didn't come back."

"Well, I can tell you what I would do. I would get just enough people to fly Discovery, maybe thirty, fill her up with food, Army rations that won't spoil, and go look for 'em."

"I don't think it's that simple."

"It would be for me. I wouldn't just leave them out there."

Aboard the Omni-Star

The ship-to-ship transmissions through NASA every six hours were routine, revealing nothing of concern. Wormhole travel could become so routine that one would not realize the staggering distances being covered per hour of ship time and per hour of lifetime of the travelers. Unless, of course, the rapid mode of transport was lost for some reason and the distances traveled had to be retraced at real time velocities.

However, there were no derelict ships sitting beside the 'road,' abandoned. No wrecks that the traffic was driving around to proceed. It seemed that the wormhole phenomenon was very reliable. Of course, if it wasn't, it would have been abandoned long ago as a flaw in space; something to avoid. The first to 'give it a try' must have been foolishly brave, perhaps foolhardy. But they handed to the other would-be travelers of the heavens a priceless gift.

Millions of miles a second

Colonel Austin leaned forward in the command chair and rubbed his back. He had begun to feel the effects of aging. Fortunately, so far, they were not debilitating; just a notice that the years had passed. NASA had already talked with him about spending some retirement time in the Zeta Spaceport in private offices as a consultant for Earth on trade and space activities. But the lure of Zeta was competing with thoughts of staying more closely connected with NASA, maybe through a position in the Star Ship Training School. Either place would be a good fit for him, and he agreed to consider both, without setting a duration for the assignment.

Then, someday, he would find himself a place in Earth's mountains, something with a front porch, a rocking chair, and a view. However, most, including himself, doubted that he could ever go from a command chair to a rocking chair.

Disaster!

As Colonel Austin jerked to a straight-up position, he almost got a kink in his sore back. The blaring alarm had shocked him back into awareness. The Master Warning Light on his command console was flashing a piercing RED and the alarm was loud enough to alert the entire crew.

There was a flurry of activity on the bridge as all hands rushed back to their positions. All essential positions throughout the ship hurriedly did systems' checks to determine the cause of the alarm. As per the Standard Emergency Procedures, all other personnel returned to their takeoff seats, buckled in and waited for instructions.

Jimmy called out for Emergency Reports:

"NAVIGATION?!"

"Nothing on the screens sir, all clear."

"ENGINE ROOM?!"

"All pods normal and ready."

"COMMUNICATIONS?!"

"All clear."

Mentar touched Jimmy's shoulder and pointed to the left side of his console. "A secondary red light has started flashing, indicating a structural failure."

Jimmy nodded. "Engineering...my panel is showing a warning light on the port side, lower level. Give me a report."

"Ah…yes, Colonel, we're checking." After a few seconds…"A Vibration Warning Indicator has activated. It appears to be the access cover to the Number 31 Port Side Proximity Sensor. Give me a few more seconds."

"Roger…standing by."

"OK, sir, we've got it isolated. Number 31 is a 12-inch square transparent cover panel, held to the ship by eight screws. Apparently, it has worked loose and is vibrating enough to set off the alarm.

If it continues to vibrate the other screws could loosen, maybe start to back out of the holes and eventually, the panel might dislodge from the ship."

Jimmy looked at those on the bridge, staring at him. He keyed his intercom. "Bruce, you were the Crew Rep in the Wormhole Characteristics class during our training… what will the dark matter do to the ship if that cover comes off?"

Bruce had already accessed the information in the computer data base. "Colonel, right now the ship is submerged in dark matter…we are totally covered with it, but it is not rubbing against the hull…no friction on the outer skin. It's merely dragging us along at billions of miles an hour. It's like we are in a huge bubble inside the mass of dark matter. The vibration seems to be caused by our ship slightly expanding and contracting along with the bubble. Looking at the stated characteristics, I'm not sure there would be any impact at all, if the cover gets dislodged. But the details are unclear in the data base. We didn't study a contingency where a piece of the ship comes off."

Jimmy keyed, "Well, maybe this is not a concern."

"Colonel."

The slightly metallic voice of Zoll came from behind. Zoll's upgrade to android capabilities did not include the synthetic voice box of Seven and the other androids.

Jimmy turned. "Yes, Zoll, do you have any information that will help us?"

"Yes, Commander, my data base tells me that this can be quite serious. That panel is on the outer edge of the port side, where the dark matter is the thickest. If the panel comes off suddenly, the dark matter could surge into the open cavity, damaging the sensor and then flow into the damaged area. If that happens, and we begin slowing for our exit at the next vortex, the dark matter may not easily release the ship. Damage to the hull could occur."

"Would the damage be catastrophic?"

"Probably not, since we would be exiting into space at a near stand-still. But there is a second possibility that also needs to be addressed."

Mentar leaned down closer to Zoll's height. "A problem with the Omni-Star?"

"No, sir, it is with Cosmos."

Bruce injected, "They are thirty minutes behind. How could this have anything to do with them?"

Zoll continued, *"If the panel becomes totally dislodged, it may just float away into the dark matter, with little impact on us. But, if it is somehow drawn into*

163

the wall of the tunnel, it will most likely ricochet off, which could slow its speed in relation to the dark matter. If the panel slows any at all, and Cosmos hits it at well over a billion miles per hour, the impact would be catastrophic."

Everyone was staring at their commander. Colonel Jimmy Austin had graduated Top Commander in his class at the Star Ship Academy. He had brought the Omni-Star through some tough spots before. He and Mentar had come through a lot together. He smiled at his giant friend.

Mentar nodded. "We think alike, old friend. You are considering deploying the Waddle Cone."

"Yes, Mentar, I think it might work."

Bruce stood. "Colonel, are you sure you want to do that? In the wormhole training they…"

"Bruce," Jimmy interrupted, "I know what they said, but sometimes a 'gut-feeling,' along with the training will make the difference. If we do nothing there could be damage to both ships." He turned to the robot, "Zoll, what will happen to the dark matter if we deploy the Cone?"

Zoll leaned into the Intercom, *"Engineering, what is the current density reading of the dark matter?"*

"The density factor is eighty-nine-point-three."

Zoll looked back at the Colonel. *"Considering the density of the dark matter, I estimate that the Waddle Cone could create a matter-free space with enough room to get someone out there to tighten the screws. However, while the hull of this ship is made of metal, hardened to withstand wormhole travel, human beings are not. Therefore, I will go out in the space the Cone creates and then repair the panel."*

Jimmy looked around at the crew and back at Zoll. "That seems to make sense. But your metal body is not as hardened as the ship."

"Yes, that is true. I could be destroyed as well. I suggest you activate the Waddle Cone and determine how much it can compress the dark matter, to create a safe working space."

Mentar added, "Zoll is right. Let's see what the Cone can do, and then decide how to proceed."

Jimmy agreed and had Bruce activate the Waddle Cone. At first there was no indication of activation, other than the green flashing light.

"First Officer," Zoll uttered, "slowly increase the Waddle Cone power to 50%. That's the maximum the engineers recommend."

Jimmy nodded for Bruce to follow Zoll's instructions. Soon the Cone Indicator was reading 50%. "Radar," Jimmy said. "What's your reading on the space created by the Cone."

"Uh...sir, the Cone appears to have opened up a 25-inch gap between the hull and the dark matter."

"WHAT!...are you sure?!"

"Yes, sir. The best I can figure, this concentrated dark matter is a lot heavier than open space. It's all the Cone can do to get 25 inches."

Jimmy looked at Mentar and they both looked at Zoll. Jimmy looked back at Bruce. "Push it to 60%."

Bruce stared. "But, sir, the engineers..."

Jimmy interrupted. "The engineers are at home, probably having dessert and watching a movie about now. They're not here, doing over a billion miles an hour in a stream of dark matter that can possibly tear this ship apart. They have the luxury of 'estimating.' We have the responsibility of doing whatever is necessary. So, advance the Cone power to 60%."

Bruce reached for the control. "Yes, sir." He dialed in 60%.

There was a slight shudder in the ship. Jimmy called out, "Radar...what's the space now?"

"37 inches!" came the answer.

Jimmy and Mentar looked at Zoll again.

The robot responded, *"It appears that my body is too thick to make it through the safe space. We will need more Waddle Cone power, or you will have to find another..."*

"I will go."

The muffled radio voice had come from behind the crew huddled around the Command Console. They turned to the voice. It was Katy Baylor, speaking from inside her EVA suit. Before they could say anything, she continued, *"I have already measured my suit and utility pack...together they are thirty and a half inches. I'm the smallest one on the crew. I will go."*

Jimmy stared for a moment, "But..."

"Sir, the longer we wait, the looser that panel becomes. I'm familiar with the tools. I can crawl from the air lock to the panel in about twenty minutes. I'll fill the screw holes with high-temp glue before I retighten them. Twenty minutes back."

Mentar leaned down. "She right. We must get this resolved and she is the most likely one to accomplish it."

Jimmy nodded. "Communications…connect me to Cosmos through the NASA link. I want to talk to Colonel Stahls."

"Roger."

In a matter of seconds, the radio link activated.

Omni-Star, this is Cosmos. I understand you have a message for me."

"Leslie, this is Jimmy. We have a potential emergency. A cover panel on a proximity sensor has vibrated loose. We have activated the Waddle Cone to create a safe space between the dark matter and the hull, so Katy Baylor can crawl out there and tighten the screws. It will take her about an hour to get it done."

"Roger, Colonel. What do you want us to do?"

"There's nothing you can do for us from thirty minutes behind. But I need you to take some actions to protect Cosmos."

"I'm listening, sir."

"First I want you to activate your Waddle Cone at 50% strength. If that panel comes off before we get it fixed, it could become floating debris inside the tunnel. If it bounces off the wall and slows down, you could hit it and destroy your ship. The Cone will protect you from the panel. If the unthinkable happens, and the Omni-Star gets severely damaged or destroyed, the Cone will be the only thing that will save you and your crew."

There was a pause of more than a few moments. "Uh…sir, that's not very likely, is it?"

"No, but if the worst is realized, there's a second thing I want you to do."

"Just name it."

Jimmy paused and looked around at Mentar and the best crew he could imagine serving with. They all understood and mentally agreed with what he was about say. "Colonel Stahls...uh, Leslie, NASA is monitoring and recording this conversation. If the worst-case scenario happens, I hereby designate you as the new Mission Commander and direct you to continue the mission to Concavia. You will recover what is left of the Omni-Star and crew and arrange for them to be returned to Earth and Zannia. Acknowledge receipt of those instructions."

After a moment of stunned silence on the bridge of the Starship Cosmos, Leslie coughed to clear the emerging lump in his throat. "Uh...roger Colonel, receipt of mission instructions acknowledged. Activating the Waddle Cone now. Good luck and God's speed, sir."

"And for you as well. Katy is headed to the airlock now. Expect to hear from us in about an hour."

"Roger, standing by."

Katy was halfway to the loose panel when she stopped a moment to rest. Her Utility Backpack was mere inches from the swirling dark matter. She lifted her head to view the thick material. She was almost mesmerized by what appeared to be shooting stars, inside the wormhole tunnel. As she focused on them, she realized that they were just tiny bits of the antimatter that made up the walls of the tunnel. They were flaking off and being consumed by the thicker dark matter. It was like a beautiful meteor shower that could only be seen from her vantage point. For a fleeting moment she realized, *"That could be me!"* She hunkered down tighter to the hull and continued to the loose panel.

By now, a third screw was loose. Using her power screwdriver, she quickly loosened each screw one at a time, added glue and then retightened them. She had it done in just over seventeen minutes. Her return to the airlock was a little faster and she finally emerged with a total EVA time of forty-seven minutes and twenty-three seconds.

When she opened the inner airlock and stood back inside the ship, hundreds from the crew were applauding. Bruce helped her remove the EVA suit.

Colonel Austin stepped up to her and shook her hand. "Katy Baylor, you are hereby designated a real live hero!" The whole crew surrounded her with handshakes and hugs for a job well done.

Mentar wrapped his huge hand around her tiny one. "Let me say to you, and the rest of the crew, at the next spaceport, your drinks are on me."

During the cheering, Melvin reached over and keyed the radio link to Cosmos. In a moment, Leslie keyed in. "Omni-Star, I take it by the cheering that Katy's mission was successful. Congratulations! We are breathing again back here. Colonel Austin, what are your instructions?"

Jimmy walked the few yards to his console and keyed in, "OK, Leslie, deactivate your Waddle Cone. Notify me immediately if you have any structure alarms that activate. In the meantime, enjoy the rest of the trip to the next vortex. Upon arrival, both maintenance teams will recheck the security of all access panels on both ships."

"Roger, Colonel, will do.

Katy Baylor was the 'hit' of the crew for the remaining time in the wormhole. She had no idea her future would include lecturing in the Emergency Actions Class at the Starship Commander's School.

Vortex

The colonel walked over to Navigation. "Melvin, what's the timing?"

"The next vortex is coming up in just over four hours. The wormhole diagram shows this junction to have the first spaceport built this deep in the galaxy, at least that they know of. The name of it is The Way Station.

"That's the name…The Way Station?"

"Yes sir. The English translation is just…**The Way Station**. It's the size of a small moon; 260 miles in diameter. It's huge. The notes say it took almost 500 years to fully complete it."

"That can mean only one thing."

"What's that?"

"There must be a lot of traffic through here from deeper in the galaxy. Otherwise, how could they afford to keep this place open? It makes me wonder what else lies on these 'super-highway' tunnels deeper in the galaxy. There's a lot we still don't know."

Melvin's eyebrows were raised. "I hadn't thought of the cost of operating these stations. How *do* they fund their existence? Zannia and Earth have traded...uh...stuff for other items. Do they just use a barter system like that for everything?"

Jimmy took out his communicator and accessed a photo of a small medallion, with strange writing and images surrounding a caricature of the galaxy in the center. He showed it to Melvin. "Seven and I discussed this subject in one of our meetings. This is the Federation's currency; it's a Digital Galaxy Note. Just like we now use International Dollars on Earth as a common digital currency among countries, they use this. Decades ago, ours was called Bitcoin.

"Zeta gave us a free ride until our upgrade to Quantum Communications enabled us to join the Federation. I had not been aware that Zeta had contacted NASA and negotiated an exchange rate for the two currencies. They did the same with Zannia. Now, whenever we use their facilities, NASA or Zannia Operations is electronically billed for our expenses."

Melvin just shook his head. "You never know what goes on behind the scenes."

Jimmy closed his communicator. "You don't think all the food and drink at Zeta was free, do you?"

"Well, I hadn't thought about it."

Jimmy smiled. "You can thank NASA for paying the bill."

Having heard their discussion Mentar wandered over to join the conversation. He smiled at the Navigator. "You Earthlings have a saying that I understood when I first heard it: 'There is no such thing as a free lunch'!"

Melvin and Jimmy laughed as they nodded.

Mentar was looking at the wormhole diagram. "Yes, that is a commonsense name. But I'm sure they still know how to bill our planets from this far out."

Jimmy nodded in agreement. "I'm guessing there is a lot to see here so I think a couple of days of Shore Leave would be beneficial for everybody. On our next stop, things will get serious. We will be sailing into the unknown. I'd like everybody to be psychologically fit and ready."

"Well, sir, like we found out at the Spirits and Song on Zeta, there's nothing like a party and a smoking drink."

Colonel Austin laughed out loud. After a few moments, he gave the arrival instructions, and both ships rotated themselves to be facing a point of light a hundred miles in the distance. A point of light accented by a backdrop of the blazing stars of the Orion Spur of the Milky Way Galaxy.

"Melvin," Colonel Austin said, amid a stone-quiet bridge, "which one of those stars is our sun?"

The navigator glanced down at his keyboard, entered a four-digit code, noted the screen, then looked back up at the windshield. "It's too small to see with the naked eye, sir."

Jimmy keyed the mic. "Navigators on both ships, activate camera magnification and route the data-feed to the heads-up display on the windshield."

After a moment, Melvin responded, "OK, that's better. Look just to the right of center, the third one down, the yellow one."

The eyes of all hands locked onto the tiny point of light for an awkward moment, then from someone behind the bridge came: "We're a long way from home."

"Not to worry," Melvin said, "I've been dropping breadcrumbs the whole way."

All eyes went from the yellow star to the navigator. Someone asked, "Breadcrumbs?"

He grinned. "I have data-locked the location of every star in this part of the galaxy. If navigation fails, I can visually know the way back. I can get us home, regardless."

"Hansel and Gretel," Jimmy said. "Ladies and gentlemen, it's been confirmed. Omni-Star's navigator graduated from elementary school."

Cosmos had been monitoring. Laughter swept through both starships.

DAN HOLT & MAX HOLT

Chapter 17

PARKING

As the Omni-Star approached the gas curtain of The Way Station, the station transmitted an automatic message to both ships, downloading the station's internal navigation tunnels and parking areas. The pilots noted that the entrance supported two-way traffic in and out of the spaceport. It was a rectangular entrance, two miles wide and one mile high.

When the entrance was 500 yards away, another starship erupted from it on their left. Some of the crew, standing at the left-hand porthole, waved at the departing ship, and got some responses. She majestically moved past the Omni-Star, and then Cosmos, slowly gaining speed.

The Omni-Star passed through the gas curtain, followed by Cosmos. Sheldon paused the Omni-Star to view the download and determine how to proceed. Cosmos pulled up beside her. The pilots, overwhelmed by the large open space that welcomed them, stared dead ahead at a landing area so vast that the entire spaceport at their last port of call would fit inside it. The download schematic matched the clearly marked moorings, laid out as orderly as a checkerboard. In between them were traffic-ways for ground vehicles, and transports, that were exiting out into the main part of the station and there were others coming in.

"Colonel," Sheldon said, viewing the landing deck a mile down and twenty miles square, "I count sixteen starships, including the two smaller ones. Where are we supposed to land?"

Jimmy looked at the schematic on the screen. He pointed. "The flashing mooring sites indicate where they want us to land. On the end of that row, two empty spaces are flashing on the schematic, so that must be where they want us to go."

Sheldon nudged the Omni-Star forward; Cosmos followed. When the Omni-Star was above the designated mooring, Sheldon engaged the Auto-Seek control of the landing system. It located the circular markings on the end-most mooring and locked on. Sheldon keyed OKAY, then Auto-Descent. The system took over and gently landed the starship on the designated mooring. A hundred and fifty-five rotor pods went to zero-thrust; a designated twenty went to Power Generation Mode. The engine room was absent the familiar hum.

Matthew Dolan, Engine Room Chief, looked at the two illuminated controls on his console, selected **Shutdown** on one and **Continue** on the other. He made the usual entry in his log and then started up the stairs. He paused half-way up to turn and visually sweep his sea of iron-angels one more time, then continued on to the main deck to check on the festivities.

Out of the corner of his eye, Colonel Austin saw Chief Dolan top the stairs and enter the main deck. He glanced at the circular rotor pod readout on the console. A hundred and fifty-five of the indicator lights were red and the remaining twenty were amber. He glanced back at the chief. "I'm going to buy him a drink," he whispered.

Sheldon Darcy happened to be close enough to hear the colonel. "Sir," he said, glancing at the chief, "I don't know those rotor pods, but I *can* drive a starship."

Jimmy laughed. "Okay, you can join the party."

Looking out the windshield, Jimmy surveyed the massive spaceport, then watched an android pull up to the Omni-Star's ramp in one of the transports. He then looked over toward at Cosmos. There was one parked in front of Cosmos as well. He looked down at the control console and keyed the radio. Cosmos responded.

"Les," Jimmy said, "As soon as pressure is equalized, and the ramps are open, go ahead and set up shore leave for everybody. We'll do the same here. I'll take an R-bot and come over there. Then let's call home."

"Yes, sir."

Frank Gordon Space Flight Center
NASA Headquarters
Communications Office

Jacob Watkins, now communications duty officer at NASA headquarters, heard the summons from the Quantum Communications receivers. It was Cosmos calling. He glanced at the clock. He'd been receiving messages from Cosmos and the Omni-Star precisely every six hours. It had been less than three hours since the last transmission. He hurried to the controls, thinking something might be wrong. He keyed transmit. "Go ahead, Cosmos."

"NASA, this is Colonel Austin. Colonel Stahls and I are calling to let you know that we have arrived at the second vortex. We are currently parked at a spaceport. This one is called The Way Station, and I must say, it's the granddaddy of all the spaceports. It's the size of a small moon, 260 miles in diameter. We are going to take a couple of days here to regroup before we travel the last leg in the wormhole. How's everything at home?"

"Everything's well here. In fact, we have a bit of news for you. The Cydonian Dome on Mars, is officially open, or, perhaps I should say, officially enclosed. It's now ready to be charged and pressurized with the oxygen/nitrogen atmosphere."

"That's great news. When we return to Earth I'll have to vacation on Mars."

"Oh, Colonel, one other thing. The President, the NASA Administrator, and Senator Stahls will be here tomorrow. I'm sure the administrator will be giving you a call.

"Thank you, Mr. Watkins. By the way, tell the Administrator that we appreciate NASA paying the bills for these trips. We've been running up quite a Tab lately."

They could hear laughter when Jacob keyed his transmitter. "Yes, sir, will do. With the whole world chipping in for this mission I'm pretty sure 'Daddy NASA' has some deep pockets."

"Roger that...I agree. This is Cosmos signing off."

Jimmy turned to Leslie. "Looks like your grandfather will be checking up on you tomorrow."

"No doubt about it," Leslie joined. "Do you remember the 'Moon letter,' the one he wrote with a giant pencil while stranded on the Moon? It's now in the museum at the Frank Gordon Spaceport. It's spread out, so you can read it through the glass."

"Yeah, I saw it. I'm still amazed at his survival."

"Me too. Grandpa is my all-time hero."

"Mine, too." Jimmy said. He then looked toward the group at the end of the ramp. His bridge crew, plus Akela, had just arrived at Cosmos ramp to group with their bridge crew for shore leave. Chief Dolan and his staff were standing among them. Apparently, someone 'spilled the beans' about the promised free drink and Cosmos' engine room staff had somehow gotten word of it.

"Come on, commander," Jimmy said, "let's check out this place."

DAN HOLT & MAX HOLT

Chapter 18

THE WAY STATION

Asked their names, the android piloting the transport for Leslie's bridge crew responded, *"I am Questor."* His colleague on the other shuttle responded with: *"In your language, my name would translate as, First."*

"First?" Colonel Austin questioned.

"Yes, sir. I was the first upgraded model produced after the android manufacturing facilities were moved here to The Way Station from our home planet."

Jimmy nodded. "That makes sense. Okay, Questor and First, take us to a lounge so we can enjoy some of that Mentar soup."

The two transports with the two bridge and engine room crews pulled away from the starships just as the line of transports began arriving to accommodate the crews of the two starships for shore leave.

When the transports left the landing deck and entered the main spaceport, the crews noticed that the general appearance of the living area was almost city-like in layout. It was not unlike driving through the streets of a typical city on Earth, including sections where there were 'cookie cutter' dwellings, identical except for different numbers superimposed on the entranceways. Well off the traffic way, there were dwellings that looked like individual houses with a vehicle parked out front, a driveway, front yard, and on one occasion, a person getting out of a vehicle and entering the front door of the dwelling.

"This appears to be an artificial world," Katy said. "It's more than just a stopover. I wonder what the population is and if many are born here and have lived here all their lives?"

"First," Jimmy said, "are there many areas like this, where people live in individual houses."

"Yes, Commander. There are two thousand square miles of living area similar to this, to accommodate the residents of The Way Station. Not far from here are some group accommodations. I think your word would be 'apartments.' Our total living capacity will accommodate almost hundred thousand individuals, depending on their physical size."

Jimmy asked, "Are there large individuals here like the giants of Zannia?"

"No, sir, at least not yet. Several species from deeper in the galaxy have individuals who have retired here but they are about half that size and smaller."

"Do these people live and work here?"

"Most of them. About twenty-two percent are retired."

Berniece Whitley spoke up. "Do they have household assistants, ah, like android maids?"

"Not all of them. Some wish to manage their own environment. Some have part time attendees. Some of the older occupants have constant assistance."

"Wow," Angie Baker said, "that's amazing."

The transports passed into an open area, made a turn, then resumed speed. Up ahead, the crews saw an aisle-side lounge on the right with a large parking area. The android chauffeurs steered the transports into the parking area. After entering, the crews selected and occupied several tables.

The girls, Katy Baylor, Sharon Millar, Angie Baker, and Berniece Whitley, talking among themselves, occupied a table together. They brought up the menu in the center of the table and made their selections. While Katy was placing her order, she saw four Athenians approaching, flying in formation. They would soon fly directly over the lounge.

Katy looked up in recognition and shouted: "KAYLAN!" The lead flyer in the formation stopped in mid-air. With his wings buzzing, he began surveying the lounge tables for the source of the voice. Katy waved her arms and called his name again. He spotted her. The thirty-inch-tall Athenian descended into the lounge, landed next to Katy, then his small arms went around her neck. Katy's eyes moistened. She gently hugged the flying creature, with one arm.

Colonel Stahls leaned over toward Jimmy. "That must be the fabled Kaylan, the Athenian. I thought he'd be bigger than that."

"You can't be a big heavy species and still fly…it's a matter of physics," Jimmy responded.

"Nature is good at physics," Leslie agreed.

Katy summoned First and he responded. Katy turned to Kaylan. "It's good to see you again." First translated. Kaylan glanced at First, then spoke: "What are you doing here, Katy Baylor from Earth. You are a long way from home."

"We are on our way to Concavia."

"Concavia?"

"Yes. We have a business matter there."

"Fourteen more lightyears from here. It must be important business."

"It is my Athenian friend. I will tell you about it someday."

"Well, you will enjoy the Grossos," Kaylan said, then stepped back a few feet to clear space for the movement of his wings. "Until next time, farewell and good luck, Katy Baylor from Earth."

"Wait!" Katy said in a raised voice, speaking above the sound of the Athenian's wings, "what are the Grossos?"

Kaylan rose four feet into the air, looked down at Katy and nodded for First to translate. "You will hear them. They sing."

Then with a smile, the Athenian rejoined his colleagues waiting in a hovering formation. He turned toward the lounge and waved once more, then the group flew away.

Hearing Kaylan's mysterious comment, Colonel Austin looked around the lounge and located Akela. He was sitting at a table about twenty feet away, having Mentar soup and talking to Dedra. She had helped the Concavian just about master the English language. Jimmy motioned, pointing toward the exile. Two of the group, sitting close to Akela, spoke to him and pointed at the commander. Akela looked around, then got to his feet and walked over.

"Yes, sir?"

"Tell us about the Grossos."

"The Concavian reacted, then took a breath. "Oh, yes, the Grossos! The best English words for them would be *sky whales*. They live in the sky. Some of them grow to be over a mile across. They are huge bags or bladders of a mixture of light gasses, living in the atmosphere. They are floaters and indigenous to Concavia. The outside surface of Concavia is an insect sanctuary or habitat of sorts. These Grossos, ah, sky whales, feed off the insects on the surface. The creatures can control their buoyancy. They float down and bait the insects with a tentacle hanging from their underbelly. It's covered with a sticky sweet substance secreted by the Grossos. When it's covered with the insects, they ascend into the stratosphere and feed off the bounty for days. When they finish eating, they sing for a day or two just like the whales in the oceans of Zannia and Earth. The song, especially those sung by the larger ones, completely circles the planet, in the atmosphere."

"Do these things go inside the planet?"

"No, Colonel. They won't even go close to the two openings located on the poles. Both poles are very cold parts of the planet. Also, the sky whales are attracted to the Ammonia-like gasses given off by the insects."

Colonel Austin studied Akela's face. "Are they dangerous?"

"No. They will think your ships are one of them. They will ignore you."

"Just the same," Colonel Austin said, "with the sky full of lifeforms bigger than my ship, we will approach with caution. Do these things, these Grossos, have a mouth."

"No."

"Good. I don't want my ship swallowed by a whale."

Mentar and his nine Zannian associates arrived on two special transports. They moved to the special area fashioned to accommodate their size. Mentar looked around when he heard his name called. One of the crew from Cosmos engine room staff spoke up. "Mentar, what size are you going to order of the Mentar Soup?"

"I think I'll try the large," Mentar said innocently, then smiled.

Laughter spread through the lounge. Mentar's group looked at him, momentarily puzzled.

The Way Station Farms

Back on the transports, the two commanders had a two-person vote and came to a decision on an itinerary: They would visit the farms, the museum, and then the Spirit's and Song.

The caravan headed for the farms that were supplying the needs of many thousands. They passed through a jungle-type area that was over a mile from entrance to exit. There were walking paths circulating through the dense growth. Next, was a prairie, complete with cactus and sagebrush.

"Everything to feel at home," Leslie said, no matter where you are from."

Jimmy said, "I wonder just how long this spaceport has been here and how much It has evolved?"

"I would say a very long time," Stahls responded. "The wormhole diagram shows it to be the very first one built."

The farms were very much a repeat of the previously visited spaceports, a complete menu of all types of fruits and vegetables, only on a much larger scale. There were acres of lush plants as far as the eye could see. An overhead artificial sun provided the heat and light needed by the plants. Dozens of androids were busily tending the crops, the gardens, and then an occasional sealed area for hydroponics. Obviously, the spaceport had been here long enough to get the nutritional endeavor down to a perfected science.

The unexpected find was that the dying plants, over the previous hundreds of years, had collectively accumulated and formed *dirt*. The grass growing in front yards was in dirt. Aside from the hydroponics areas, the gardens and fields were growing in dirt. Jimmy asked for and was granted samples of this special dirt to return to Earth for study.

There was one established fact common to all spaceports and all starships; no animals allowed. All space travelers had to be vegetarians. The advent of space travel gave rise to the science of creative dishes made with vegetables only. The growing of animals for food was not supportable in a closed environment. Some starships would leave port with sizable stores of meats that had been prepared for cooking and serving and were loaded in a frozen state. They were enjoyed, of course, but, when depleted, they reverted to a vegetarian diet. Many that became starship crewmembers, launched as meat eaters, but arrived home as vegetarians.

The Museum

Leaving the farms behind and moving on to the museum brought a surprise. The first exhibit was an Athenian shuttle, the smallest of the functional excursion ships. Apparently, the Athenians freely represented themselves in the world of the space faring.

But then, the second exhibit, the second shuttle, was eighteen feet in diameter, eight feet high, and sitting on its three-legged landing gear with the ramp open. Akela saw it and stopped abruptly. "A Concavian shuttle!" he exclaimed. He spontaneously went up the ramp and seated himself at the controls and looked at the group through the windshield.

"Are you a pilot?" Colonel Austin asked.

"Yes," Akela responded, rubbing the console of the ship. "However, it's been a long time since I piloted a ship." He got up from the pilot's chair and came down the ramp, then walked all the way around the shuttle, laying his hand on it.

"Akela," Colonel Austin said, "what kind of power?"

"It's inertial, Commander."

Jimmy looked around the group and located Dedra, from records, and motioned her front and center. She looked up at the colonel. "Yes, sir?"

"Dedra," he said, "I need for you to do something for me. You are familiar with the wheel clusters that power the Zannian shuttles, aren't you?"

"Yes, sir."

You are small enough that you can enter the Concavian ship. Go inside it and look at the wheel clusters and see if they are like the ones in the Zannian ships."

Dedra looked down at Akela, smiled, then went up the ramp and into the Concavian shuttle. Akela followed her into the cabin, stepped around her and raised the cover of one of the wheel clusters. Dedra examined it. "Yes, sir. It's smaller, but it's the same configuration, wheels in the middle of wheels, with the offset centers."

Akela closed the cover, then turned to the console and began pointing out the controls and explaining them to Dedra. She was smiling and nodding. Colonel Austin smiled, then addressed First. "How long has this Concavian shuttle been here?"

"This exhibit dates just over two hundred years ago."

"Is this ship still operational?"

"Yes, Commander. All exhibits in the museum are maintained operational."

"I wonder if they have updated their propulsion. This craft is over 200 years old."

"Maybe," Leslie agreed.

"We'll see."

Jimmy stepped over into the aisle, then looked back along the line of transports. "Has Snyder and Abbott and Cosmos' DOE crews got here yet? I want them to see this Concavian ship and to look it over in detail."

Dedra and Akela noticed the activity outside the shuttle and rejoined the group. The word was passed back several transports to the one occupied by the DOE pilots and their crews. Their chauffeur steered the transport to the center of the aisle and proceeded to the shuttle exhibit. Colonel Austin waved them over to it.

"Gentlemen, this is a Concavian ship. I want you to look it over. Same power as the Zannian shuttles, as far as we know. One thing though, this ship is over 200 years old."

The DOE crews circled the ship, studying its profile. Captain Snyder stuck his head and shoulders through the entrance to the cockpit, went down on one knee and studied the controls, then looked around at the cabin. Abbott and the two pilots from Cosmos did the same.

"Interesting," Snyder said. "I understand that they are a very advanced civilization. They may have something much more powerful now."

"We'll see," Jimmy said.

For the next two hours the crews of starships Omni-Star and Cosmos enjoyed the exhibits of many various examples of equipment designed for the business of space exploration. All of them addressed the three essentials, oxygen, gravity, and atmospheric pressure, in a variety of ways.

In the Spirits and Song Club

The building that housed the Spirits and Song Club at The Way Station was more than twice the size of the Zeta branch. The club system had spread throughout the wormhole system long before man had learned to fly. It was learned from the older androids that Spirits and Song clubs were in all spaceports. There was such organization throughout the galaxy, waiting for lots of younger worlds to grow up.

As the occupants of the two Earth ships began pouring into the club, several androids were taking chairs from the tabletops and setting them back on the floor. Apparently, they had just finished a major cleaning of the entertainment center. They carefully cleaned the miniscule amounts of soil that had been either tracked from the spaceport's farms or brought by some patron from a distant planet. Colonel Austin wondered if, perhaps, someone aboard one of Earth's starships had brought a little piece of Kansas to Zeta or Procyon 2. He figured it all belongs to the same galaxy.

Jimmy looked across the sea of tables, noting that there were varying sizes, giving the establishment a three-dimensional look. There was a bar that went all the way across the front of the main room. Stools lined it. There must have been a hundred, with a third of them occupied. They varied in size and height. On the right, as in Zeta, there was a stage on which musicians could perform; only this one was much larger. This Spirits and Song here would seat over a thousand, perhaps considerably more. Some sections of the wall appeared to be movable partitions. He seated himself along with his bridge crew and some of his technical people. An android appeared to wait on those already seated as the remainder of the ship's crews filed in.

Soon, drinks were being set in front of the group. The tiny spirals of smoke marked the standard drink of the Spirit's and Song system, unless specified differently. The minutes turned into an hour, then two. Gradually, the group of over a hundred, grew quiet. Rumblings began to be passed one group to another, then individual to individual. Bruce Wilson, first officer, was the first to say it out loud. "Colonel, everybody's ready to go."

"Go?" Jimmy questioned, although he knew what was being inferred.

"On to Concavia, sir."

"There's one more vortex and one more spaceport on our way, at the Concavian end."

"We can hit it on the way back, when we leave Concavia. That's what everybody is saying. We—they—want to get there. Hearing about the Grossos sparked everybody's desire to get there. Everybody wants to spend our time moving toward Concavia until we're there."

Colonel Austin paused only seconds. They had planned to spend two days here so continuous flight from now until arrival would make only make a two-day difference in actual transit time. But it was the crew's motivation that ruled. "Okay, everybody to the ships." He sought out the android. "First, I want you to take Colonel Stahls and myself to the main offices of The Way Station. I want to thank them for this special place and their hospitality, then, please take us to our ships. He turned to Bruce, "Make sure everybody is accounted for and safely aboard ship. Relay the same to Colonel Stahls' Executive Officer."

"Yes, sir, will do."

There was a mass exodus from the Spirit's and Song, returning to their ships for immediate departure, though they were guests of The Way Station for less than a day. First made arrangements for a four-seat vehicle for transport to the main offices, sixty miles away. He and the two Commanders boarded it and proceeded to the nearest elevator two miles away, then were whisked to the crown of the spaceport and to the main offices.

Jimmy and Leslie entered the receptionist's area and were seated. Minutes later, an older gentleman, slightly stooped, and white-haired, entered the seating area and extended his hand, smiling.

"Sir," Jimmy said, staring at a seemingly familiar face, "you look a lot like Tholan, the Station Master at Zeta."

The older stationmaster smiled and nodded. "He's my son. I'm Maalan."

"Well," Jimmy said, taking his hand, "it's a small galaxy. I wanted to thank you for an excellent stopover, and your staff's hospitality."

"You're welcome, Commander. Visit any time. The word is, you are on your way to Concavia."

Jimmy nodded. Maalan continued: "Just for your information, Commander, the Concavians are a very technical society. They are blunt, and straightforward when interacting with you. They do not engage in niceties, etiquette, or pleasantries. They will speak point blank to you and want you to do the same. They are not ugly about it; that's just who they are. To be kind is very awkward for them."

Jimmy and Leslie looked at each other. Jimmy replied, "Thanks for the heads up. We appreciate it. Our Concavian passenger seems to be an exception to that. But he has been gone from there for 26 years. I guess those passing through Zeta had a positive influence on him. We'll be sailing on shortly. Thanks again for the hospitality."

"All hands present and accounted for," Bruce reported. "Cosmos reports everyone on board."

"Very well," Colonel Austin said. "Power up the ships and begin departure procedures."

Thirty-five minutes later, the Omni-Star and Cosmos, released their moorings. Half an hour later, the two ships exited the spaceport and began to gain speed toward the vortex. After contacting NASA, the Omni-Star entered the wormhole. Next stop...the Concavian Vortex. Thirty minutes later, Cosmos did likewise. Fourteen days and they would be at the final wormhole vortex before setting sail for their final destination - the planet Concavia, and the answer mankind had sought since the beginning.

.

Having settled in at their billions-of-miles-an-hour speed in the wormhole, Colonel Austin leaned forward and rubbed his back, then rotated his shoulders and neck. Bruce Wilson, noticing the Colonel's discomfort, stepped over to the console, keyed medical and spoke to them privately. After a moment, he stepped over close to the commander. "Colonel," he said quietly, "why don't you go to medical and let our physical therapist check your back."

Jimmy turned and shook his head, "N0, I'm alright."

"I know, sir. I just noticed you rubbing your back. A lot of our department heads experience back pain from sitting too long without moving around. It's rarely debilitating but I know firsthand it can be very annoying. Glenda Winsor, down in Medical, specializes in spinal decompression. I was talking to her not long ago and since we have had the artificial gravity system installed, she has a couple dozen of the crew that come to her with back issues. She says it's because the crew doesn't experience weightlessness like we did before.

Therefore, there's no relief on the spinal column. The gravity keeps it under constant pressure. You should go to medical and let her adjust your spine. Chief Dolan leaves the engine room and goes to her once a week."

"He does?"

"Yes, sir. He says it works wonders with his back."

"Well, maybe I'll check it out."

"Good idea, sir. I'll take over for you."

"Now?"

"Yes, sir. She's waiting for you."

Jimmy looked up at Bruce, who was smiling disarmingly. Jimmy got up and headed for Medical and therapist Winsor. When he walked into the medical department, Glenda was waiting. She handed the Colonel a medical gown and pointed at a small dressing room. "Remove your jumpsuit and put on this gown, then lie down on the examining table, face down."

"There's nothing wrong with me," Jimmy said, as if the therapist hadn't heard that before.

"I know, Colonel. I reviewed your medical record. You're a lucky man. You have enjoyed exceptionally good health. I want to decompress your spine to allow good circulation between your vertebrae. We have had quite a few cases, more than usual, of back pain since artificial gravity was installed on the Omni-Star."

Jimmy changed into the medical gown and laid down on the examining table. The therapist opened the gown down to his waist, then began examining his vertebrae one at a time, pushing each one from side to side, then exerting straight on pressure. She employed some type of device that vibrated the vertebrae individually, then she adjusted them again. Jimmy, With the restored circulation, Jimmy experienced a feeling of euphoria.

"How's that?" the therapist inquired.

"I don't believe it!" Jimmy confessed, sitting up on the examination table and twisting and rotating his shoulders. "My back feels great!"

"Colonel, I want you in here once a week."

"Yes ma'am."

DAN HOLT & MAX HOLT

Chapter 19

TRAPPIST 1

T he Omni-Star moved a mile to the side of the exit from the wormhole tunnel in the final vortex to wait for Cosmos. She appeared as expected. Colonel Austin ordered the two ships to move well away from the vortex, and to hover at Station Keeping power. He then ordered a revied of ships' status, having just finished an additional two weeks in the wormhole system.

In the distance, some fifty miles away, was a yet-unexplored spaceport. As the portal to the Trappist 1 system, it was most likely staffed by Concavians. Radar and sensor monitoring assessed the spaceport to be about fifty miles in diameter. The Wormhole Data Charts listed it be only a hundred years younger than The Way Station.

The general sentiment of the crews was to 'push-on' and visit this stopover on the way back to Earth. After almost a year and a half of ship-time, from Earth to Concavia and back to this vortex, a stopover and shore leave would, no doubt, be welcome.

Barring any emergencies, onboard ship time can eventually get boring. The crew facilities included restaurant-looking dining halls, a large library, several gyms full of the latest exercise equipment, a modern style coffee shop, apply named, 'Higher Grounds,' two movie theaters and multiple lounges for sitting and talking or just watching the star systems go by. There were TVs in the lounges with current programming being downloaded via the Quantum Communications Data Band. However, a popular pastime was to watch the TV signals that had come through open space, showing programming that was, at this point, fourteen years old.

NASA's Electronics Division was working to expand the Quantum Communications Data Bandwidth to enable real-time video back to Earth from Concavia. They were on track to finish the modification in time for the arrival of the starships at Concavia. As a bonus, the entire world would be able to watch the broadcast from the hollow planet.

The ships left the vortex behind, assumed their formation flying positions and began the final leg of the mission. Now, the longest leg of the journey, timewise, was underway. The total time in the wormhole system, counting the stops was forty-five days. This stint would be just under a year. As the chronometer marched on, the ships' companies gradually settled in for the duration.

Colonel Austin's mind went to Brad Givens, the cowboy from the 1800's who was abducted by the ancient Altairians and rescued from their wrecked ship. By now he had arrived on Zannia and was probably trying to figure out how to resume life with his extended family some four or five generations removed.

Jimmy walked over to Communications. "Patch me through to Jeremy Weston on Zannia."

"Yes, sir. Standby."

As he waited, he took a moment to marvel at the incredible Quantum Communications System. Without it there would probably be no Federation of Planets. In less that a minute an answer came.

"Hello, Omni Star. This is Weston."

"Jeremy, this is Colonel Austin Is your grandfather available?"

Spaceport maintenance shop
Zannia

Jeremy looked up at his grandfather across the shop floor at a training table where he was working with two other trainees dismantling a rotor pod. Jeremy had gotten into the habit of referring to his grandfather from the remote past as 'Givens' to smooth their interaction in the day-to-day vigil of training. It had become routine with the training crew.

"Givens," Jeremy said loudly, "it's for you."

Brad looked up, laid down a spanner, wiped his hands, and took the communicator. "Hello, this is Givens."

Colonel Austin paused only seconds, then quickly adjusted. "Brad, this is Colonel Austin aboard the Omni-Star. I was just wondering how you were doing in your new job on Zannia."

"Great! I'm just getting started with the training, but just great!" Then Brad turned away from his colleagues and spoke with a quietened voice: "Colonel, my

201

grandson is scary smart. I'm proud of him. And these rotor pods are fascinating to work with. Life's good here. How about you and the people on that ship. Did you find what you were looking for?"

"Yes, we did. We are on our way there right now."

"I'm glad, Colonel. Well, I'd better get back to work. The boss wants to know why this rotor pod is out of balance."

Jimmy smiled. "Understood. Just learn to work at Jeremy's level and you'll be fine."

"That's my goal. Well, Goodbye, Colonel. Thanks for calling."

Goodbye Brad."

The Final Leg

Colonel Austin's mind left Zannia and returned to the quest. Small group planning meetings were happening almost daily on both ships.

Colonel Austin signaled Mentar. "Mentar, Zoll could be a great help upon our arrival. How about sending him to the Records Office and have Dedra program him to speak the Concavian derivation of Italian."

"Will do, Colonel," Mentar said, then instructed his mechanical assistant to go and be programmed to speak ancient Italian.

When Dedra was alerted that Zoll was on his way to be programmed to speak Italian, she paged Akela to come to her office. Then she searched for the special cable connection she would need. The robot was now android-capable but still had the older input connections.

When Zoll arrived, Dedra had requested maintenance to bring platform to Records. When it arrived, she boarded it with the electronic translating and programming device in hand. She looked up at the robot/android. "Zoll, pick me up and hold me near the access ports in your chest."

Zoll reached down and picked up the platform and records specialists and held her at waist height. Dedra opened the panel on Zoll's chest and plugged in her device, then activated it. Seconds later it signaled transfer complete. She looked up at Zoll's large face. "You're smarter now, you can put me down."

Zoll carefully set the platform with mezzanine cage and Dedra back onto the floor. Dedra turned to Akela. "Verify his Italian. Speak in Concavian and tell him to translate it into English for me."

Akela smiled and nodded, then looked up at the android and spoke two sentences in the language of the hollow world ahead. Zoll turned to Dedra. "Thank you for everything you have done to help me prepare to come home. I would like for you to meet my family."

Dedra smiled, "It was my pleasure. I would love to meet them."

Zoll turned to Akela and translated her response into Italian.

"He's got it," Akela said, smiling.

As the hours, days, and weeks rolled by, many of the crew visited with Akela, with Zoll's assistance, discussing his childhood memories and experiences. They were searching for the *feel* of life on Concavia, hoping for a better chance of success interacting with the government officials concerning their quest.

The scientists on board were using this opportunity, provided by this mission, to study the heavens from this new perspective. Both telescopes were busy around the clock. It was planned that on the deceleration phase of the last leg of their approach to Trappist 1, that the aft telescope of the Omni-Star, which would be forward facing during that phase, would be trained on Concavia's star to wait for the seven planets to be close enough for detailed viewing. They had learned during the research at Zeta's library that the Trappist 1 system just had Concavia in the, so called, Goldilocks Zone, and all the other six were barren, frozen, wastelands orbiting far from the parent star. The outermost planets in the system were near a half lightyear from Trappist 1. The scientists aboard the Omni-Star, with its special equipment, were hoping for close flybys of the planets that happened to be near the line of flight on the approach to Concavia.

Chapter 20

THE STAR SYSTEM

The pin-dot of light appeared in every monitor on the Omni-Star and Cosmos. All eyes of the crews were locked on it, watching it slowly brighten. They had crossed three of the outer planets' orbits, the planets themselves having been on the other side of the star, slowly obeying the laws of orbital science, laws that would keep them away for hundreds of years. Planet four of the seven was close to the flight path of the armada. To the delight of the scientists on board, she would be roughly the same distance as the Moon is to the Earth, at her closest point to the ship. The scientists were busily checking focal length and tracking numbers. Navigation reported that there was a sensor array on Concavia that was monitoring their approach to the Trappist 1 system.

Radar had reported that Concavia had gigantic quantum communications antennas in geostationary orbits above both poles. Obviously, it was the only way the population could communicate from inside 250 miles of solid rock. It would also make their first contact with the planet easier.

Colonel Austin addressed the bridge. "Okay, they know we are here. How long until arrival?"

Melvin Faulkner answered. "Twenty-one days, three hours. We will come to a hover one hundred miles above the surface of the planet."

Jimmy stared at the orange image of Trappist 1 through the windshield for a long moment. Though it was a cooler star, a dwarf, proximity had now made it the brightest in the windshield. He said, almost to himself, "I wonder if that is enough clearance."

"Sir?" Melvin asked.

"A hundred miles. This planet has a mean diameter of 12,000 miles. We know the surface is a sanctuary for insects which grow prolifically. And the sky is filled with huge lifeforms, the Grossos. I'm wondering just how far above the planet the atmosphere extends."

"That's a good point, Colonel," Melvin said. "The planet does have dual atmospheres. According to our research, the one inside is roughly eighty-twenty N_2/O_2 and the one on the outside surface is near the same, but heavy in ammonia. It will be interesting to see what mechanism keeps them separate."

"What would we need to do," Colonel Austin continued, "is double that hundred miles altitude upon arriving at zero velocity?"

Melvin turned to his navigation computer. His fingers danced on the keyboard for just over a minute. "Okay, Colonel, there are two ways to make the change and arrive at Station Keeping two hundred miles above the planet. One, increase engine thrust ten percent for twenty-eight minutes, then go back to normal 1G deceleration. And two, alter our trajectory by point-zero-one-six of a degree. The curvature of the planet will give us the extra altitude. We will arrive two hundred miles above the planet. A note, sir, if you choose to increase power temporarily, everybody on board will gain about twenty pounds for twenty-eight minutes. That could create issues here and there in the ship, perhaps in medical."

"Point well taken," Mr. Faulkner. Contact Cosmos and have their and our computer teams review a trajectory change to gain the extra altitude."

"Yes, sir."

Katy Baylor and Sharon Millar were already looking at the numbers. They contacted Cosmos. Soon, Melvin, Katy, Sharon, Walter, Henry, and Berniece were in a digital round-table to ready a program to enter into both starships' main computers and add an additional hundred miles altitude to their arrival position in Concavia's atmosphere.

They contacted both engine room chiefs and requested that they video-attend the meeting to be savvy to what was about to be asked of the starship's engines. It would be a course change with the two half-mile-wide vessels flying within a thousand feet of each other. The meeting was all about maintaining that safety clearance. Changing course was easy, simply turn the 'steering wheel,' so to speak. The challenge would be changing course with two vessels, each with a mass of thousands of tons, exactly in unison, and in perfect proximity of each other.

Less than an hour later, following two flawless simulations, Melvin addressed the colonel. "Sir, we have the program for the new course ready to activate."

Colonel Austin looked out the windshield toward Trappist 1. "Engage, Mr. Faulkner."

A 'gong' sounded throughout both ships. All knew it's meaning and postured themselves to await the event. Thirty seconds later, there was a faint nudge of the ship as the engines moved the zero velocity point several hundred miles, to arrive at predetermined point that was still three weeks away.

Chapter 21

CONCAVIA

Hover Point
Altitude - 200 Miles

Upon arrival at the hover point, Colonel Austin keyed the Intercom. "Navigation; unlink the computers to allow both ships to maneuver separately. Communications; establish a permanent intercom link between the Omni-Star and Cosmos for the duration of our visit here at Concavia. I want everyone informed as the events occur, whatever they may be. When you finish that, start working on the quantum video link to NASA. They can relay to the White House and whoever else they want to watch the historic moment when we finally meet the Concavians. Also engineer a link to Zannia Headquarters. Everyone needs to be in the loop. This is what every human on Earth has been waiting for."

"Yes, sir, will do."

Mentar looked at Jimmy, "And Zannians too."

"Yes, my friend, we are all in this together. Everyone needs to see Concavia and witness our interaction with the ones who can finally answer life's basic question: Where did we come from?"

Mentar hesitated. "I just hope we are all ready for the answer."

Jimmy nodded reflectively. After a moment, he keyed the mic again. "Cosmos; monitor this comm-link continuously until further notice. Quantum video and audio links to Earth and Zannia are being established now."

"Roger, Colonel."

Having overseen the initial setup for their arrival, Jimmy walked to the massive windshield and joined the bulk of the bridge crew, gathered to see firsthand this strange world. He stepped over and looked down at Akela, who was staring in amazement and pointing as he narrated for those standing nearby. Akela's command of English had continued to improve, and he was describing the planet below to all who would listen. Finally, he sensed that Jimmy was observing him.

He looked up and smiled. "Home!" he said.

Jimmy smiled back. "Yes, I know what it's like to go home. Let's just hope your government officials are a forgiving lot. What will you do first if they say yes?"

Akela thought for a moment. "My family, they have no clue I am here. My exile punishment prevented me from communicating with them. My wife, my children...uh, my children are all on their own by now. I want to see them first. My wife is a strong mate, she would have never given up on me returning. Then I want to eat some fresh Zuntilapon. My wife makes the best on the planet."

"Zuntilapon?"

"Colonel, it is the best stuff you'll ever put in your mouth. It reminds me a little of Mentar soup, except it has a lot of seasoning and extra vegetables in it...the kind you can only find here on Concavia. If all works out, I want you to meet my family."

"Yes, my friend, I know how important family is; I would love to meet them."

Bruce walked up by Jimmy. "Colonel; look at this." He was pointing to the nearest video monitor, displaying a large structure 500 miles directly above them. Jimmy squinted. "What is it?"

"Engineering identified it as some sort of radar tracking antenna, about 50 miles in diameter. It is in a geo-synchronized orbit."

"Fifty miles wide?! It's gotta be for deep space tracking. It's obvious...they know we are here."

"I wonder why they haven't hailed us yet. I've been expecting it."

Jimmy nodded, "Yes, me too. Maybe they're waiting for us to approach the entrance. I will initiate contact when we get closer. Right now, I want to take a close look at the outer planet."

Communications hailed Jimmy on the overhead intercom speaker. "Colonel, we have the video link to Earth. It's on the monitor at your console."

Jimmy walked to his console and sat, looking at the President and the NASA Director, together in the Oval Office. He keyed the mic. "Mr. President, we have arrived at Concavia. We have not yet made contact

211

with the inhabitants. We are observing and scanning the planet to record everything for the archives. We plan to keep this channel open throughout our visit here."

The President spoke. "What about Zannia, are they in the loop.?"

Mentar had walked over when Jimmy was paged. He leaned into the President's view. "Yes, Mr. President, my planet is in contact; we have them on an adjacent monitor. I'm told that Jack & Brenda Owenby have all your Earth colonists assembled in the headquarters to watch history unfold. I trust the citizens of Earth will be informed as events unfold."

"Yes, Mentar, video feeds have been offered to all the countries with monitor capabilities. No one will be able to contact you directly…only through NASA's primary link. Your mission will also be displayed on all the major public screens on Earth, like the big one in Times Square. "

Jimmy responded. "Thank you, sir. Now, if you'll pardon me, we have some work to do here before official contact is made."

"Yes, Colonel, of course. God speed…stay safe."

When Jimmy stepped over to the adjacent monitor, Mentar was talking to Kronos on Zannia. When he saw Jimmy step into view, Kronos smiled. "Colonel, greetings from Zannia! We are excited about your encounter with the Concavians. Your teacher and cowboy are doing well getting acclimated to life in Little

One City. They will be watching your encounter with the Concavians, along with the rest of us."

"Yes, Kronos, give my best to them."

Mentar finished his conversation with Kronos and joined Jimmy back at the windshield. Akela had his nose against the glass, looking down.

"It looks like a normal planet," Bruce Wilson said.

They were all looking out at pale blue space, hanging above the darker atmosphere of the light grey planet, whose surface was curving away into the distance. At 200 miles altitude, the eye could not make out any small details on the surface.

Jimmy stepped to the console. Melvin looked up from his monitor.

"Colonel, the course change put us over the equator. You can't see the gateways to the interior from this vantage point. According to the information gathered in Zeta's library, the gateways are exactly on the poles of Concavia. Also, the planet's spin-axis is perpendicular to its sun. That means that their sun never shines into the interior of the planet." He hesitated. "That must be why they created the sphere; the artificial sun."

Yeah, that makes sense," Jimmy said. "How far to a gateway?"

"Flying at this altitude, about ten thousand miles. Five hours. We are about the same distance from the two gateways or poles of the planet."

Jimmy turned and motioned to Akela. When he came over, Jimmy asked, "When we get permission to enter, will it make a difference which portal we enter?"

"No, Colonel, the government headquarters is located equally from both portals." He started to go but turned after a few steps. "By the way...those fluffy white clouds...they're the Grossos."

"Thanks." Jimmy turned to the First Officer. "Bruce, take us down to 100 miles altitude. Let's have a closer look."

The Grossos

All eyes on both ships were looking down on the planet's surface; it seemed to be alive. Earth and Zannia were also watching. The giant sky whales, although their size unable to be appreciated at this altitude, were lazily bobbing up and down in the atmosphere. The scene seemed animated.

Colonel Austin looked over at Akela standing at the windshield staring at his home. "Mr. Antonyo?"

"Yes, sir?" Akela said, turning to face the commander.

"I'm sure the Concavians know we are here. How would they feel about us flying among the Grossos and imaging them for our scientists aboard and those back home, as well as all the people of Earth?"

"They would expect it, Commander. It's a common practice."

"Apparently, they are not worried about foul play; someone trying to steal one of them or something."

"No, sir, the size of the Grossos protects them. Many of them are over a mile in diameter. A few are almost two miles across. There was one incident, long ago, where a larger ship came and tried to capture one of the babies about 200 feet wide. The Concavian government sent out two fighters. The ship broke off, apologized, and left."

"Who was it?" Jimmy asked.

"I don't know." Akela responded. "The government sealed the record of the incident. They must have made some kind of a deal with that planet. Talk circulated around the communities that the Concavians received some serious compensation to downplay the event."

The Cosmos intercom keyed in. "Colonel Austin, shall we descend further?" Colonel Stahls said. "I'm curious about these animals, floating animals, no less, like hot air balloons back on Earth."

Colonel Austin gave Leslie's suggestion the nod and Sheldon Darcy, pilot Omni-Star and Dave Walters, pilot Cosmos began to descend flying abreast of each other. The ships slowly sank into the realm of the Grossos, the sky whales, filling the air above Concavia.

"Sir," navigation reported, "two of them are coming up beside us starboard. They're huge; a mile and a half across! They could swallow both of these ships!"

"They don't have mouths," Jimmy said. "I checked."

Momentarily, the ship was filled with a very low-pitched musical note that was held for minutes. Then it changed to a higher pitch, then back down.

"Omni-Star," Leslie said excitedly, "are you picking up that whale song?!"

"Yes," Jimmy said. "I think the hull of the ship is picking it up from the atmosphere."

Howard Wiggins, Starman, was standing at the starboard porthole observing the gigantic indigenous animals, listening to the pure deep bass sounds echoing through the ship. He breathed words of appreciation. "What magnificent creatures," he whispered, then stepped over to the nearest intercom terminal. "Colonel Austin, may we board a shuttle and get some close-up images of these wonderful creatures. Sir, we'll be very careful not to hurt them or frighten them. We need detailed documentation to take back home."

"We are already recording the whale song into the archives," Dedra reported.

Jimmy was quiet for a moment, then replied. "Colonel Stahls, what do you think?"

"They are so special and so rare, and when would we ever come this way again. I would like to have documentation if it can be done without causing an incident or unduly disturbing the animals."

"We'll be very careful," Howard interjected.

"Commander," Akela said, "I'd like to go with them. It's been a long time since I've seen the Grossos up close. I can point out some things for the scientists."

"Very well," Jimmy said and then keyed the mic. "Troy Fennell, power up Shuttle One. Take your navigator and three of the scientists and their equipment. Your will have a tour guide; Akela will be joining you."

"Mr. Fennell," Colonel Austin added, "exercise due caution. Keep all your maneuvers slow and smooth. As small as you are, they should ignore you. However, you are larger than most of the insects they catch, so if the Grossos should notice you and become interested, return directly to the ship."

"Don't worry, sir. If they get the idea that I'm a tasty insect and start moving that long sticky tentacle toward me, I'll beat it back to the ship. Leave the doors open on my hangar."

Jimmy smiled. "Will do."

Howard, occupying the center seat of the shuttle, finished prepping his recording and imaging equipment. His eyes went to the windshield just as Troy steered around the Omni-Star and came face to face with one of the football-shaped, sky whales. The sheer size of the lifeform was overwhelming. As the shuttle approached, still a mile away, he could see the translucent skin of the Grossos. It looked like an amber colored membrane about six inches thick. Toward the ends of its football shape, the color gradually turned orange. The *nubs*, the two ends of its bodily shape, looked like the nose of a dirigible, multiplied by a factor of ten. The ends themselves were half a mile across. Veins, like blood veins, could be seen webbed throughout the body of the creature with various colors of liquid inside them.

There was an appendage hanging from the underbelly of the animal. It was about three feet in diameter and a mile long, getting larger near its end. About halfway down, there were thousands of insects glued to its surface. They were covered over by some type of white webbing, like a spider web.

"That must be lunch," Troy said.

"Beautiful, aren't they," Akela said. "Mr. Fennell, descend down toward the bottom of the creature, then slowly approach. I want to show you something."

Troy steered the shuttle downward about a half mile, then began a slow approach toward where the tentacle connected to the main body of the Grossos. Details soon became discernable. There was a rectangular-shaped growth on the bottom center of the creature. The appendage came out of the center of it. Forward, toward the point of the body shape there were enormous eyes, two of them, side by side, looking almost straight downward. Each was fifty feet across with about that much distance between them.

"I don't believe it!" Troy's navigator said, "they are huge!".

"Let's move in a little closer," Howard said, "so I can get some detailed images of them. They are fantastic."

Troy slowly inched the ship toward the face of the sky whale. When the ship passed within a thousand feet of the creature, the eyes slowly opened. The eyelids, with a black coloration, slowly slid from over the pupils that were also black. They fronted on a white eyeball of enormous size. The eyes rotated a few degrees and focused on the shuttlecraft. Troy eased his hand up on the console and flipped the cover from over the Emergency Power button and left his hand over it. The huge eyes followed the small ship for about thirty seconds, then went back to center and the lids closed.

Troy started breathing again and closed the cover of the emergency control. "Colonel," he reported, "this whale opened its eyes, enormous eyes, and looked at us for a few seconds and then apparently went back to sleep."

"Back to sleep? Good; I think I know why. I'll bet these things judge their altitude by the magnetic lines of the planet and your ship has a strong magnetic signature. It's system probably picked up your unusual signature and it took a look. Fortunately, that was all."

"Colonel," Howard interjected, "the eyes have a blank look about them. These creatures are not sentient. There's a large number of them below us, maybe a thousand feet lower in the atmosphere. Could we descend and image them?"

"Go ahead, shuttlecraft, we'll follow you. Stay alert."

Troy began a slow descent. In viewing the sky full of the creatures, there seem to be three groups of the sky whales, at three distinct levels. At the higher level there were many of all sizes. They seemed to be sleeping and feeding at the same time. At the middle level, the creatures had their appendage rolled up against their underbelly and were lazily rocking end to end of their oblong football shape. At the lowest level, where the appendage was lying on the ground among the insects, there seemed to be the numbers about equal to those at the highest level.

"The middle level are the ones that are singing. There are fewer of them than at the other two levels," Howard observed.

"Maybe the very young haven't been to choir practice yet, and the elderly have given up the ritual," Troy offered.

"Makes sense, Mr. Fennel," Jimmy responded.

Howard was quiet for a few moments, studying the Grossos. "It appears that they go down, capture the insects for food, ascend close to the stratosphere to sleep and consume them at the same time. Then when they've finished, they descend deeper into the atmosphere, medium level, and sing. What marvelous creatures. Did the Concavians create this ecology?"

"Yes," Akela said. "It was their first project, eons ago."

"I'll give them this," Howard said, "It's a smashing success."

"Colonel,' Howard said. "We've got to check out the details on the surface below us. The records at Zeta indicate that the Concavians are the third civilization to occupy this planet."

"We'll see about that after we make contact. I don't want our close approach to be seen as an aggressive maneuver."

Chapter 22

CONTACT

Jimmy keyed the mic. "Cosmos…follow us to the portal and we'll make contact."

"Roger."

Both ships ascended to just above the middle level of Grossos and flew in the direction of what they determined to be the North Pole, and the opening to the interior of the planet. With all cameras pointed at the surface, they were able to see some obvious signs of Concavia's history.

The Zeta files had revealed that throughout many millennia, other civilizations had occupied Concavia for undetermined lengths of time and then abandoned it. The cameras were now recording evidence of previous occupations. Remnants of severely deteriorated cities and infrastructure, roads and bridges, were obvious. All were either overgrown by vegetation or covered by a thick layer of insects.

Three hours into the flight toward the portal, Jimmy looked over. "Bruce, increase altitude back to 200 miles and bring us to a hover when we get over the opening. We will attempt contact there."

"Roger, sir. I'll coordinate with Cosmos."

Starting about 500 miles out from the portal, the cameras were capturing the changing landscape and the changing sky. The grossos became fewer and fewer. The planet's outer surface slowly became almost totally devoid of the big insects. The surface gradually transformed into a cold, lightly snow-covered landscape.

Finally, the Omni-Star and Cosmos were side by side, facing the 500-mile-wide opening into the unique hollow world. Colonel Austin paused, looked around the bridge, and the keyed the radio. "Planet Concavia, this is the Starship Omni-Star, come in please."

There was a pause. Both ships were silent in anticipation. Jimmy was about to key the radio again when it came alive.

"Omni-Star, you are speaking English, an Earth language."

"Yes, both starships, the Omni-Star and Cosmos, are from Earth. Our crews consist of representatives from both Earth and the planet Zannia. We have journeyed far to beseech an audience with your scientists."

"We have been aware of your approach since you entered the Trappist 1 System. What is the purpose of your request? What do you seek?"

"We search for our birthplace, our history and our beginnings. We traced our origin on Earth to the giants of Zannia. Then, joining them, we traced the giants of Zannia to you, Concavia."

"Omni-Star, you are not the first to come to Concavia with such questions. We will allow you entrance, and an

audience with our scientists. The answers they supply may not be what you want or hope, but they will be the truth. Wait where you are."

The radios went silent for a few minutes, then the instructions continued.

"Omni-Star, you and your accompanying ship may enter the portal. When you exit inside, an escort will be waiting. Follow it to the science pavilion. Land there."

"Acknowledged," Colonel Austin responded, deliberately maintaining few words in his communications, as per the advice from The Way Station.

DAN HOLT & MAX HOLT

Chapter 23

THE HOLLOW WORLD

The massive ships smoothly began the descent into the portal. They entered within a mile of the side wall of the tunnel. The difference was obvious, going from the brightness of the Concavian sky into the darker reaches of the portal. The movement of their ships began to activate motion detectors imbedded in the walls, turning on huge floodlights to light their way.

The two pilots spotted the gaseous curtain dead ahead, sealing the interior of this world with its atmosphere, from the harsh outside world belonging to the insects and their regulators, the Grossos. From a thousand miles away, the curtain of gas would appear to be a giant milky eye of the planet or a lake some 500 miles across and perfectly round, surrounded by a white barrier of encrusted ice and snow, a no-man's land between the insect world and the hollow world.

It looked the same as the gates at the spaceports. Jimmy marveled at the incredible technology of the Concavians to construct such a gateway across a span of 500 miles.

Members of the crew were crowded around every window, porthole, and view monitor as the Omni-Star and Cosmos cruised the final 100 miles inside the portal. Akela stood with eyes glued to the windshield. Soon, everyone could see that the walls were covered in a green growth of some kind, sprinkled with reds, yellows and purples. The colorful blossoms seemed to be tacking the green growth to the walls. When they broke into the light of Concavia, the beauty was breathtaking. The inside of the planet/geode was almost like a lush tropical garden. Small rivers laced the landscape, their origins were unclear.

The metal sphere, hanging 5,000 miles away in the center of Concavian's inner space, projected a bright glow, lighting up the surface below. Sensors on the ships detected no harmful UV rays from the artificial sun. Its light was gentle and warm to the surface of the ships.

The inside diameter of the planet, being just shy of 12,000 miles made the surface look completely level. But, if one looked forward to the horizon, the upward-arching surface of the inner-planet could almost cause vertigo for the crews, who had only traversed planets with the surface curving down and away from them. When magnified, the feed from the top camera, looking some 12,000 miles straight, up showed the planet's opposite inner surface, with rivers flowing, dwellings, and forests. Depending on the orientation of one's mind, it seemed that the water in the rivers, millions of tons, could come crashing down on them at any time. But the spin of the planet kept it all in place.

The down-facing cameras brought into view the nearest town to the opening, over a hundred miles below. Marble-looking columns and white spires dominated the small town.

Bruce Wilson did a video and voice check with Earth and Zannia. Both were still in good contact. He was impressed with the quantum antennas the Concavians had placed in space above the openings to their planet.

Shortly, a female voice from the radio alerted Jimmy. *"Omni-Star, I am Quintalia of the Concavia Visitor Control Center. You will see my shuttle off to your right front. Please follow me, one ship behind the other. We will remain in the transit-speed lanes, at four thousand feet, aa you measure distance on Earth."*

Visitor **Control** Center, Jimmy reflected. "Roger, Quintalia, we see your shuttle. We will follow."

The three ships, in-trail, proceeded toward the center of the planet's governmental headquarters city, approximately 10,000 miles away. The Welcome Shuttle set a speed of 5,000 miles an hour, giving the crews of the visiting ships time to observe their planet, a scenic tour of sorts. Everything they were seeing, and recording seemed to be either new or very well preserved.

"There it is! There it is!" Akela was pointing and yelling. Others rushed to the windshield.

"What is it?" Dedra asked."

Akela placed both hands on the glass and looked down as the armada passed over the area. "Home!" Then he looked up with a small tear visible in the corner of one eye. "My village, my home, my family."

With moist eyes, Dedra placed her hand on his shoulder. Jimmy stepped over. "My friend, we will do whatever we can to secure your place back here where you belong. Remember, our offer of asylum on Earth for you and your family is still good, if your government isn't in the forgiving mood. Either way, you will be with your family."

The tear in Akela's eye completed its trip down his cheek. "Thanks, Commander."

The scenes of beauty and newness were repeated in every area of Concavia the ships passed over. Finally, the armada slowed and followed the shuttle into an approach to the large tarmac, adjacent to what was obviously the Science Pavilion. There were large antennas on top of the buildings and the construction seemed to be of a glistening metal, rather than the stone construction of the villages they had flown over.

In a few minutes, both ships settled onto their landing gears. The landing surface was also made of the same pristine smooth metal that constructed the science buildings. Melvin keyed the intercom. "Colonel, the atmosphere scan shows it to be very much like Earth...normal Oh2 levels."

"Roger. Mentar and I will exit and greet the delegation. Our discussion with them will determine who else we will need from the crew. Akela, you stay out of sight until I call you. Communications, we are ready for our body cameras. Cosmos; install yours as well and standby."

There was a few-minutes delay in opening the air locks to the outside, as Jimmy and both bridge crews were fitted with the small cameras that would transmit back to the ships, to be relayed to Earth and Zannia. Finally, all was ready.

When Jimmy stepped off the ramp of the Omni-Star onto Concavia, he went airborne for about 10 feet, almost falling when he landed back on the surface. Mentar's experience was almost as comical. He helped steady Jimmy and then smiled. "We forgot about the gravity generators. We just stepped from Earth gravity into Moon-level gravity."

Jimmy recovered, feeling embarrassed in front of the waiting Concavian delegation. Somewhat out of character, the Concavians had allowed a slight smile. While returning the smile, he keyed his communicator and told the bridge to warn all aboard of the differential in gravity strength. For a moment, it donned on him that perhaps billions of people had witnessed the most ungraceful exit he had ever made from a starship. He put that aside and continued toward the waiting group of scientists and government officials. They were all diminutive in stature, like Akela.

Mentar and Jimmy stopped a few feet from the waiting group. There was an awkward moment as the two mature space travelers from many lightyears away, seemed unsure how to proceed. The Concavians stood motionless, content to wait. Finally, Jimmy spoke, "Colonel Jimmy Austin of Earth and Mentar of Zannia, request permission to inquire of your scientists.

We have questions that we on our planets have pondered for eons."

The obvious leader of the waiting group stepped forward and addressed them, in perfect English.

"Colonel Austin, I am Dekaton, designated authority on Concavia. My position is roughly equivalent to your country's President on Earth. It has been well over a year since we learned of your intention to visit our planet and ask your probing questions. The debate among us has been ongoing and sometimes heated. Some scientists here believe we were unwise to allow you through the portal into our world. They feel that allowing your visit is a waste of our time. Still others feel that we have been misunderstood and misrepresented to the galaxy at large and that it is time to explain. That group seems to have won out. So, in the name of Concavian leadership, let me welcome you."

Mentar said, "Thank you Mr. President."

Jimmy followed. "Yes, we are grateful for this opportunity. While we seek information from you, we have aboard, one Akela Antonyo, a Concavian citizen, who is seeking clemency to return to his home."

"We have known of Akela's presence on your ship since you arrived at The Way Station and are aware of Earth granting of asylum to him. Bring him forth; clemency awaits him on Concavia."

As Jimmy turned to inform Akela, he was already standing at the top of the ramp. Halfway down, Dekaton passed by Jimmy and walked up the ramp to meet him with the normal Concavian friend greeting. *"Welcome home, teacher."*

After the traditional arm-shake greeting, the two continued down the ramp to Jimmy's questioning look.

Akela asked, "Dekaton, how long have you been the leader?"

"Five years. Many younger politicians and scientists have taken over from the older generation. It was your leadership of the protests against the seeding of worlds that resulted in the population eventually demanding a change to our scientific genetic experiments. In many ways, I owe my leadership appointment to you."

Jimmy was listening, with his mouth partially open. "Wait...do you two know each other?"

Akela smiled. "Yes. Prior to my arrest, I was a schoolteacher in my village. Dekaton was one of my students in my Politics Class. He was the smartest and had the most reasonable approach to controlling the scientific community, which had been running the government for generations."

Jimmy said, "Wait, I thought you said you were a pilot."

Akela nodded, "Yes. All schoolteachers were required to be shuttle pilots, so we could provide the transportation for our students doing research. I believe on Earth you call them *field trips.*"

Dekaton added, *"Akela's concern about the out-of-control seeding of worlds was felt by many others in our society but most were afraid to stand up for that belief. When he organized and led the protests, the government decided to stop them by making an example of him. You know the rest."*

Mentar chimed in, "But, how did you know he was on the Omni-Star?"

"We have an ambassador who resides at The Way Station. He communicated to us about Akela the day you arrived there."

"What took so long for that attitude to change? He was at Zeta for 26 years."

"Change takes time. I and others from Akela's time as teacher, had to grow into adults and work through the higher education system to slowly change the attitude of the leaders.

Jimmy responded, "Thank you, Mr. President, for allowing Akela to come home. We have on board something that belongs to you. We would like to return it."

"What is it?"

Jimmy gave the order and Zoll and four Zannians appeared, carried the Moai down the ramp, and stood it up on the tarmac.

The dignitaries and scientists gathered around the pattern statue, examining it.

"You found this on Earth?!"

Mentar nodded. "It was in some ancient, abandoned ruins in the mountains on Earth. Earth's scientists now suspect it was part of a failed experiment, they just don't know what."

Dekaton was smiling. *"This,"* he said, *"is the answer we have been seeking."* He turned to a scientist in his group and spoke in a dialect that even Akela did not understand. The group nodded and turned toward the large science building.

The leader turned back. *"All aboard your vessels may disembark at their leisure. We have prepared some welcome refreshments for all of you. You, and any of your crew you desire, may come with me to the Science Pavilion for an explanation. Also, we will address the questions you have for us. I hope you will not find the answers disappointing."* He turned toward the building.

Akela said, "Wait. What about my family? When can I go home.?"

"Dekaton pointed toward the building. *"See that citizen holding the door open for us? That's your son, Galen. Your wife and daughter are waiting inside."*

Akela's eyes welled up with tears. He embraced Dekaton.

"Welcome home, my friend."

The whole group, including many of the crew who had disembarked, filed into the huge science building, with 50-foot ceilings, occupying over 50,000 square feet of space. There was already a celebration of sorts underway. Akela had a protracted and emotional reunion with his family. Jimmy bent down to receive a hug from Akela's wife, who tearfully thanked him for bringing him home. She expressed a desire to one day journey to Earth to thank humanity and the giants for the vision to search other worlds for the answers to their origins. Jimmy assured her that she and Akela would be most welcome on Earth anytime.

After a short time, Dekaton called for the group to follow him to the Concavian Archives. The head scientist led the way to where there were rooms and hallways filled with artifacts and depictions of hundreds of worlds from across the galaxy. They proceeded to an inner set of double doors.

Inside the large semi-circular room was a series of different statues mounted on pedestals. Everyone stepped forward to survey the displays. They were all different depictions of beings carved in stone.

Dekaton explained. *"These statues are master patterns of sentient beings on seeded planets."*

Jimmy looked at Dekaton and said, "What is the significance of the statue we returned? Why was it on Earth?"

The leader explained. *"Many thousands of years ago, a small group of renegade scientists wanted to manipulate DNA to create species, not for scientific research, but as warriors and servants, that could help them take over parts of the galaxy by force and create their own kingdom. Their plan was discovered, and the ancients of our planet marshaled a force to stop them. They fled Concavia in two ships containing this stolen statue and the amber fluid necessary for sentience. Our scientists feared their plan was to plant the statue as a pattern for the beings they wanted to create on their target planet. Obviously, this proves their target was Earth and that they failed, and that the amber fluid was lost. The ancient archives do not reveal the details. But, we have always feared their return, possibly with an army of servant warriors."*

Mentar spoke, "The amber fluid was not lost."

Dekaton looked at Mentar, *"What do you mean?"*

Mentar continued, "The archives of our ancient escape ship, Zannia 2, record that as the ship was in route to Earth's solar system, it encountered a ship adrift; a ship with the remains of an ancient crew, apparently lost long ago, and a cargo of large bottles of amber fluid. The fluid was transferred to the Zannia 2 and the crew of the derelict ship was given a proper space burial."

"I am glad to hear the matter is closed.

Jimmy spoke. "Dekaton, we have returned your statue. We have also returned your teacher. Now, for our questions."

Dekaton smiled. *"Ah, yes, the questions that you and so many others want answered. Although I know what they are, you may ask them now."*

Jimmy looked at Mentar. It donned on both of them that they had never decided in detail how to verbalize the questions that all of their species had been asking for eons.

When neither of them responded immediately, Katy Baylor spoke up. "Your scientists have been manipulating DNA and designing species for eons, right?"

"Yes, unfortunately, they did."

"Are you, uh…" she hesitated, swallowed, then finding her voice, spoke firmly: "Are you what some would call God?"

Dekaton, hearing the depth and gravity in the Earth woman's voice, and viewing the countenance on the faces of the visitors from Earth and Zannia, spoke directly to the point. *"We have gotten that question many times. The answer is...No. We manipulated...but we have never created. We do not have the ability to create."*

Jimmy leaned forward a little. "Then, who did...where did life come from...where did we come from?"

Dekaton measured his words. *"We don't know. All we know is that the Universe springs forth life...life of many kinds...life in many places. We find it everywhere. There may have been a beginning, a time from lifelessness to life, but, in our experience, we cannot know that. And we, being what many call a pragmatic species, do not see it as important to our future.*

"We discovered the, so called, amber liquid by trial and error in our research with DNA. We found that it enhances the basics that come with life, the instincts that cause survival, the search for food, teamwork for protection, colonizing, until the net result is keen awareness. We found it worked on humanoid platforms; the simian branch of bipeds.

"Now, just in the last one hundred of your Earth years, you have traveled many trillions of miles and accomplished things that other species have never imagined. You think that knowing your beginning will direct you toward some future destiny. But the fact that your quest brought you to our hollow world in less than 100 years is incredible. Other species have taken thousands of years to darken our door. You two, humans and giants, are cut form the same strain of DNA. You are

indeed special species. You are the ones who will decide your path forward. We envy you. You are young in the exploration of who you really are and who you want to eventually become. I predict that your kinds will have a far-reaching impact on our galaxy, and maybe eventually on the Universe.

"So, my advice to you is this...never stop asking the deep questions. Use the passion I see in all of you to pursue the answers, no matter where in the Universe they may take you. You have many adventures yet to experience. Go forth from here and explore every question. The next time you look in a mirror, realize that you are looking at an eternal mystery. With that realization, teach those who follow you to embrace who they are and to never lose the excitement of being...life."

There was an extended hush in the room...and all over two planets many lightyears from here. The crews of the Omni-Star and Cosmos were looking at each other with a renewed admiration for what they had accomplished. This, and everything up until now, had knit them into a team...a family of giants and humans, that would transcend the variations of DNA. Jimmy and Mentar looked at each for the first time...as brothers.

Jimmy knew two things to be true; after today, he would never be the same, and he would never have been able to fully explain this to the billions on Earth and Zannia, had they not been watching the video-feed for the past few hours.

DAN HOLT & MAX HOLT

Chapter 24

HOME

The quantum video feeds to Earth and Zannia had both planets in a state of continuous celebration. While many question marks remained, the basic answers to life's pressing questions had been answered.

The NASA television channel was rebroadcasting the events around the Earth, 24/7. On Zannia, engineers quickly electronically connected view panels across the planet, creating Zannia's first television network. As the new Headmaster of the Earth Colony School on Zannia, Lilah Owenby used many of the video clips to teach the understanding and tolerance of other species and cultures. Jack and Brenda were beaming with pride at the maturity of their grown-up granddaughter.

The Concavian government held a conference with all officials and scientists to establish in writing an agreement that they would adhere to interstellar principles of respect for other species and non-interference in the cultures of others. In a show of support and appreciation, Jimmy and Mentar signed the document as witnesses to the agreement.

Finally, after a week of combined research on Concavia, the crews of the Omni-Star and Cosmos had boarded their ships and were powering all systems, preparing to launch from this amazing hollow world. Jimmy and Mentar stood at the bottom of the ramp, reluctantly saying goodbye. Dekaton and his staff gathered to say farewell, along with Akela and his family.

After some handshakes and a few awkward hugs, the crews of both starships were onboard and ready for launch. Jimmy stood at the windshield of Omni-Star, looking at the farewell delegation. They raised their hands in an Earth-style 'goodbye' gesture. Jimmy looked at Mentar. He smiled. Then, they both came to attention and rendered a slow salute.

A year and a half later
Home Again

The Omni-Star and Cosmos exited the wormhole vortex into the solar system. The long trip home to Earth had been spent by each crew member in preparation for what would happen next in their lives and careers. The experienced crews would be sought after by NASA to provide expert advice in their areas of experience as the fleet of star ships continued to grow.

Mentar and Jimmy had spent many hours together, reminiscing about their adventures and the close-calls and emergencies they had dealt with along the way. Because of them, member planets in the Federation had gained a new respect for the newest planets to join the organization.

During one of their conversations, Mentar asked, "So, will Earth continue to explore, now that your initial purpose seems to have been met?"

Jimmy nodded. "Yes. Once mankind has been given a taste of the unknown, he is difficult to satisfy. Don't be surprised if you see bigger, better and faster ships than the Omni-Star, hurling through the galaxy in the near future. Someday...who knows...maybe the first intergalactic mission may be a combined crew from Zannia and Earth."

Mentar smiled. "If I were younger, I'd like to be on that ship."

Jimmy nodded, "Yeah, me too." Then he asked, "So, how will you occupy your time in retirement on Earth?"

Mentar paused and then smiled. "Kronos is now an experienced leader of Zannia. His leadership and young ideas will move Zannia to new heights in the Federation community. I do not need to concern myself with my home planet. And my son will be on Earth soon. I will finally get to spend quality time with him. I petitioned NASA to enroll him in their next Star Ship Training class. He will start as a Navigator on the next ship Earth commissions."

Jimmy smiled. "I feel certain Menvaar will make an outstanding navigator."

Then, in a moment of seriousness, Mentar said, "My friend, I require just one future promise from you."

"Anything, Mentar, just name it."

The giant hesitated. "Jimmy, I'm a hundred and thirty-two. When I no longer breathe, promise that you will return me to my longest residence, with my students who did not survive on the Moon. I want my name added to the Memorial Plaque."

Jimmy swallowed hard. He put his hand on the giant's huge arm. "I promise."

Mentar continued. "And I am keeping Zoll as my assistant until that time comes. Then, I trust you will find a useful place for him."

Jimmy nodded, "Consider it done."

Two days later, Dedra entered the bridge and asked for Colonel Austin. "He's on the engine deck," she was told. She took the elevator down and walked toward the Maintenance Chief's Office. In route, she noticed the Colonel a few yards down one of the side passageways. She turned and approached, noticing he had his hand on the casing of a rotor pod.

He smiled. "Here, put your hand on the casing. Feel that? This amazing invention, developed in a garage, decades ago, has taken us to the stars. Whatever comes next to replace it, will never have the...uh...character and personality of these rotor pods."

Dedra felt the slight vibration and heard the low hum of the amazing magnetic power source. "Yes," she said, "I can see how a commander could get attached to a machine like this." She paused, "Uh...sir, the reason I came looking for you is to ask for your approval for..."

Jimmy took his hand off the rotor pod and smiled, "Your request is approved."

"But sir, how could you know that…"

"That you have requested entry into the Starship Commander School? I heard, and I approve your request. You will make a fine commander someday."

"But, sir, I just wanted your endorsement. The final approval will have to come from the General who is the Director of the Star Ship Command School."

Still smiling, he said, "Yes, I know…and I approve your request."

Dedra stared at the colonel. "You?! You're the new Director?!"

"Yes. After I transition command of the Omni-Star to soon-to-be Colonel Bruce Wilson, I will be promoted to General and will assume the role as Director of Star Ship Commander training. You will be a student in my first class."

Her smile broadened. "Sir, there could be no better Star Ship Commander to learn from." Then she thought, "But what about flying into space. I know how much you love it, and you are the best commander I can imagine. Won't you miss it?"

"Actually, no. I will still fly on all training missions and I will be developing our own Wormhole Training Division. So, I will travel often to Zeta and even back to Zannia. I will also be an adviser to the construction company soon to be selected to build the future space station at the Kuiper Belt Vortex."

Then he smiled broadly. "But it is you and the future crop of commanders who will really stretch the legs of our fleet. I will be cheering you on as you explore worlds we have yet to even discover." He pointed to the wall of the Omni-Star. "There...out there, there are incredible discoveries to be made. You, Commander, have an exciting life ahead of you. Back in the Zeta Library, do you remember that we found Malcore, the planet orbiting a red dwarf star?"

"Yes, sir."

"Unless my timing is wrong, you will be one of the First Officers assigned to be the Number Two onboard the next ship to explore that unknown world. It is somehow connected to the pyramids of Giza...we just don't know how. I will be looking to you to unravel that mystery. Not long after that, I can see you commanding your own ship."

Dedra took on a look of great respect for the commander who had brought her to this place in her life. She stepped back a few feet, came to attention and saluted. Colonel Jimmy Austin smiled, came to attention and returned the salute. Then, he added a hug.

Two Years Later

NASA Starship Commander's School

Graduation Day

Lieutenant Colonel Dedra Allison couldn't suppress her rapid heartbeat and radiant smile as she held the diploma in her left hand and gripped the right hand of the Colonel recognizing each graduate. She released his hand and snapped a sharp salute, then did a left-face and preceded to stage-right, off the stage and through the double doors into the Reception. Inside, the Commandant, Brigadier General James Austin waited to give a final congratulations to those who completed the rigorous training. As he returned her salute, he smiled. "Congratulations, Dedra, I'm proud of you; Number One in your class. Why am I not surprised?"

"Thank you, sir. I am grateful for your recommendation to be First Officer on the Omni-Star. Colonel Nolan sent me a note, welcoming me to the crew. He is due back from the Zannia 2 ship next week, when the trainees finish their Ship Egress training."

"Well, you earned the second position on the bridge. Learn well from Bruce and I will look forward to someday pinning the Colonel eagles on your collar. That new ship may someday be *your* ship. Has the Omni-Star crew been given the transfer date yet?"

"Yes, sir. The Quantum Alpha will be ready for space trials sixty days from today. I was at the assembly plant yesterday. They just put the finishing touches on the crew quarters. The ship is a third bigger than the Omni-Star. The new Q-Pods have been online for over a week. The Quantum Crystal that the engineers incorporated in the design has stabilized the rotor pods like never before. Sir, you should lay your hand on the casing and listen…it's the sweetest hum you've ever heard."

Jimmy smiled, "Getting hooked already, I see. That happens. And it's hard to beat the added open space velocity and the double escape velocity when you're in a tight spot. To space junkies like us, it's more than a machine...it's a living-breathing part of our world. There's nothing like it. I'm glad I had a hand in designing the upgrade."

"Didn't you design the new Cone too."

"No, that was Kronos and his engineer team on Zannia. I just greased the wheels here to get it done in time for Quantum Alpha's first mission."

"Well, I'll feel safer on the Q-A knowing the Waddle Cone will create a shield twice as big as before. The wormhole system can't take us everywhere, so the open space capability of the new ship will be very important to our space exploration. I can't wait to try it out."

Jimmy smiled, "Test it well. The Universe is waiting."

AND THE JOURNEY CONTINUES!

ABOUT THE AUTHORS
(Update as of 2020)

Sadly, **Dan Holt,** author of Underneath the Moon, Books One – Six, passed away in 2019. (He had completed the 'shell' of Book 7, which his brother Max will attempt to complete and publish.) He was a U.S. Army veteran, having served three years as a Communications Specialist in Germany. He spent the remainder of his civilian career as a self-taught engineer, designing and testing large-scale production equipment for the file-folder industry. The efficiency and durability of his designs even garnered interest from some foreign manufacturers.

In retirement, Dan used his writing skills to express his continuing fascination with science fiction. His variety in sci-fi thought is also evident in his other novels, SLEEP MODE and KEEPSAKE. The Underneath the Moon series, Sleep Mode and Keepsake are all now available on audio through www.audible.com. See all of Dan's books at the publisher's website, www.maxholtmedia.com.

Max Holt is a retired U.S. Army pilot, having served 22 years on active duty, including two combat tours in Vietnam. He is an avid science fiction reader and writer. Max started his publishing company, Max Holt Media, in 2015. This book continues Max's partnership with his brother, Dan Holt, to write more of the UNDERNEATH THE MOON saga. Max has released Book One of a new series, entitled...AI RISING. Book One...THE DOME, was released in 2017.

Max has two sons and six grandchildren. He enjoys playing Bluegrass Music, traveling and has collected flags from 39 countries. Other than the USA, his favorites have been Switzerland, Austria, Italy and the UK, where he has established a life-long friendship with a family in Darlington, England. He now lives in Mount Juliet, near Nashville, Tennessee.

Contact Max: www.maxholtmedia.com
                          vietnampilot22@gmail.com
On Twitter - @maxholtmedia

Other Sci-Fi books by Max Holt:
Alien Planet